Praise for the 13 Reasons for Murder Series

"…hard to put down and am keen to read the next in the series."—Reader's Favorite 5-Star

"Full of sass, good friends, and a bit of blood, this novel was a joy to read."—Julie E.

"…suspenseful, addictive…hope there are more books with this character."—BookBub Review

"I look forward to…learning more about Britney."—Studiohnh.com Review

"…oddly addictive…cannot wait for the next book…"—Amazon.ca Review

"…flows at a quick pace and leaves you wanting more…" —Goodreads Review

"The plot is fresh and unique, a nice change to read something a little different…"—Reader's Favorite 4-Star

"…well written and kept me on the edge of my seat…"—Heather W.

13 Reasons for Murder Haunt

13 Reasons for Murder #9

Amanda Byrd

Blacksheep Press LLC

Contents

About the
Author

Amanda Byrd is obsessed with fictional serial killers. From Patrick Bateman to Dr. Hannibal Lecter to Dexter Morgan and every butcher in between, Amanda loves figuring out what drives fiction's deadliest monsters. When she's not busy writing, Amanda can be found reading, playing video games, or watching shows and movies like Mindhunter, Hannibal, and Dexter. She lives in Florida with her bloodthirsty, flesh-eating cat.

Follow Amanda online
www.amandabyrd.net

Sign up for my newsletter and get a free story

Follow Amanda online:
Facebook: Author Amanda Byrd
Instagram: amanda_byrd_author
Goodreads: Amanda Byrd
Bookbub: Amanda Byrd

One

THE SALT AIR WHIPPED through my hair as we headed back to shore, the engine humming beneath us. I couldn't stop smiling. Not the fake, forced smiles I'd perfected over the years, but something genuine. Something real.

Stu's hand found mine as he steered with the other, and I squeezed it tight. We'd done it together. Katie was gone, and the rush I felt wasn't just from the kill—it was from sharing it with him. From knowing that he understood me completely. No judgment. No horror. Just acceptance of who I really was.

"Feel better?" he asked, glancing at me with those dark eyes that had seen me at my absolute worst and somehow loved me anyway.

"More than better," I said, leaning back against the seat. "I feel. . . complete."

And I did. For the first time since Dario, maybe even longer, I felt like all the pieces had finally clicked into place. The therapy sessions with Ben had helped me understand my past, but this—this was my present. My future.

The dock came into view, and I felt a slight pang of disappointment that our night was ending. But then again, this wasn't really an ending, was it? This was just the beginning.

We secured the boat in relative silence, both of us still riding the high of what we'd accomplished together. It wasn't until we were driving home that either of us spoke again.

"So," Stu said, his voice casual but I could hear the undercurrent of excitement, "how long until you get that itch again?"

I laughed, surprising myself. "I don't know. Maybe sooner than usual. Sharing it with you. . . it's different."

He nodded, understanding exactly what I meant. That was the thing about Stu—he got me.

We pulled into our driveway, and I noticed the old cunt across the street peeking through her curtains again. Seventy-something, widowed, and with way too much time on her hands. She'd been watching us for months now, and I was starting to wonder if she suspected something or if she was just a lonely old bat with nothing better to do.

"She's at it again," I muttered, nodding toward the house.

Stu followed my gaze and chuckled. "Maybe she has a crush on me."

"Or maybe she's nosier than she should be for her own good."

The words hung in the air between us, and I saw Stu's expression shift slightly. Not disapproval, exactly, but a question.

"You're not thinking—"

"No," I said quickly, though the idea had crossed my mind more than once. "She's too close to home. Too risky. We've been through this."

But as we headed inside, I couldn't shake the feeling that the old cunt might become a problem. People who watched too closely had a way of complicating things.

I pushed the thought aside as we got ready for bed. Tonight had been perfect, and I wasn't going to let paranoia ruin it. Stu and I fell asleep tangled together, and for once, my dreams were peaceful.

The next morning my alarm dragged me back to reality. Work. Responsibilities. The mask I wore for everyone else.

I dragged myself out of bed and went through my morning routine—coffee over three ice cubes, exactly the way I liked it, while my laptop booted up. Stu had already left for his shift, kissing me goodbye with a lingering touch that reminded me of everything we'd shared the night before.

I was halfway through checking emails when my phone buzzed. Unknown number.

Saw the announcement in the paper. Can't wait to check out Nightmares Unleashed! Finally, someone who understands real horror. —J

I stared at the message, coffee growing cold. Nightmares Unleashed. I'd heard about it—some new horror attraction opening next month. Like Halloween Horror Nights, but local.

I'd been curious about it, actually. Horror attractions were something of a guilty pleasure for me. The irony wasn't lost on me that someone who created real nightmares would enjoy fake ones.

But this text. . . something about it felt wrong. Invasive. How had they gotten my number? And why did they think I'd care about their horror attraction?

I deleted the message and tried to focus on work, but I couldn't shake the feeling that something was off. This felt personal in a way that made my blood simmer. People who invaded my space, who assumed they knew me—they had a way of pissing me off beyond reason.

By lunch, I'd googled Nightmares Unleashed and found myself falling down a rabbit hole of information. James Wylder, the creator, was some hotshot designer who'd worked for major theme parks before striking out on his own. The attraction was supposed to be "immersive horror like you've never experienced"—whatever that meant.

But as I dug deeper, reading interviews and promotional materials, something twisted in my stomach. The scenarios Wylder described, the "realistic" approach to psychological horror. . . it hit too close to home.

One interview made my hands clench:

"We're not interested in cheap scares or gore for the sake of gore," Wylder explained. "What we're creating is a psychological journey that taps into real trauma, real fear. We want people to experience what it feels like to be truly helpless, to understand what it means to be at the mercy of someone who enjoys causing pain. It's cathartic, in a way. It helps people process their own experiences with abuse and manipulation."

I slammed my laptop shut so hard I was surprised the screen didn't crack.

Cathartic. Process their experiences.

This asshole was making money off people's pain, turning trauma into entertainment. He was taking real horror and packaging it for thrills.

My phone buzzed again. Another unknown number.

You should come to the preview event next week. I think you'd really appreciate what we're trying to do here. —James

This time, I didn't delete the message. I screenshot it and sent it to Stu with one word: *Problem.*

His response came back immediately: *On my way home.*

I spent the rest of the afternoon researching James Wylder. Age fifty-two, divorced, no kids. Lived alone in a house about twenty minutes from here. No criminal record, but that didn't mean anything. Some of the worst monsters I'd ever known had clean records.

The more I read about Nightmares Unleashed, the angrier I got. This wasn't just some harmless haunted house. Wylder was advertising it as "therapeutic horror," claiming it could help people work through trauma by experiencing controlled terror.

Bullshit.

I knew what real trauma looked like. I'd lived it with Dario, and I'd seen it in my victims' eyes. It wasn't something you packaged and sold for twenty dollars a ticket.

By the time Stu got home, I was pacing the kitchen like a caged animal.

"Tell me," he said simply, setting his keys on the counter.

I showed him everything. The texts, the interviews, the promotional materials. I watched his face carefully as he read, looking for any sign that he didn't understand why this was so important.

But of course he understood. That was why I loved him.

"So what are you thinking?" he asked when he finished reading.

"I'm thinking James Wylder needs to learn what real horror feels like."

Stu nodded slowly. "When?"

"Soon. After that preview event. After I can see exactly what this sick fuck has created. I need to experience it myself first."

"You want me to help?"

The question made my heart race. Having Stu with me for Katie had been incredible, but this felt different. More personal. This wasn't just about the kill—this was about sending a message.

"Not directly," I said. "But I might need backup. This one's going to be more complicated."

Stu leaned against the counter, studying me. "What makes him so special? I mean, besides the obvious."

I was quiet for a moment, trying to find the words. "He's profiting off pain. Taking something sacred—the kind of fear that changes you, marks you—and turning it into a joke. Entertainment."

"And that pisses you off."

"It more than pisses me off. It makes me want to show him what real fear looks like. What it means to be helpless."

The words came out sharper than I'd intended, and I realized how much this had gotten under my skin. James Wylder didn't just represent another kill—he represented everything I hated about people who turned real horror into a game.

My phone buzzed again. Third unknown number of the day.

Can't wait to see you at the preview. It's going to be unforgettable. —Your biggest fan

I showed the message to Stu, and I saw his jaw tighten.

"He's playing games," he said.

"Yeah, well. I'm better at games than he is."

That night, I couldn't sleep. Every time I closed my eyes, I saw Wylder's promotional photos—his smug smile, his confident pose, the way he talked about trauma like it was just another tool in his kit.

I found myself thinking about Dario, about the way he'd used my vulnerabilities against me. About how long it took me to understand that what he'd done wasn't love—it was systematic destruction disguised as romance.

And now this asshole wanted to recreate that feeling for paying customers.

I slipped out of bed, careful not to wake Stu, and padded down to the kitchen. I made myself coffee even though it was two in the morning, and I opened my laptop again.

Time to learn everything there was to know about James Wylder.

His social media was a goldmine. Photos from the construction site of Nightmares Unleashed, behind-the-scenes glimpses of the "sets" he was creating, proud posts about his "groundbreaking approach to experiential horror."

In one video, he walked through what looked like a replica of a therapist's office, explaining how visitors would be "guided through a psychological breakdown that mirrors real therapeutic processes."

I wanted to put my fist through the screen.

But as I kept scrolling, I started to see patterns. Wylder wasn't just some entrepreneur looking for a quick buck. He was obsessed with this project. Several posts mentioned his "research" into trauma and abuse. Others hinted at his own experiences with "psychological manipulation."

And then I found it—a post from six months ago that made everything click.

Sometimes the best way to heal from trauma is to confront it head-on. To take control of the narrative and turn your pain into power. Nightmares Unleashed isn't just an attraction—it's my therapy, and soon it can be yours too.

The accompanying photo showed Wylder standing in what looked like a recreation of a domestic violence scene, complete with overturned furniture and broken glass.

I felt sick.

This wasn't about entertainment or even profiting off pain. This was about a broken man trying to work through his own issues by forcing others to experience his trauma.

Which made it worse.

I closed the laptop and finished my coffee in the dark, planning. James Wylder thought he understood horror, thought he could package it and control it.

I was going to show him how wrong he was.

The preview event was in five days. That gave me enough time to attend it, experience whatever sick fantasy Wylder had created, and then learn his routines, map out his house, figure out the best way to get to him.

But first, I needed to see Nightmares Unleashed for myself. I needed to understand exactly what I was dealing with, let him think he was safe in his little controlled environment, before I showed him what real control looked like.

As I headed back upstairs, I felt that familiar tingle. The hunt was beginning, and this time, it was personal.

James Wylder was about to learn that some nightmares couldn't be controlled.

And some monsters weren't content to stay in the dark.

Two

THE NEXT FEW DAYS fell into a strange rhythm. On the surface, everything looked normal—I went to the office, handled client calls, dealt with temp placements and interviews while Barb managed the front desk. But underneath, my mind was constantly churning over James Wylder and his sick little project.

I'd become obsessed with researching Nightmares Unleashed, but I had to be careful. Too much digging from my office computer could leave traces, and the last thing I needed was Barb or Julie wondering why the owner of a temp agency was so interested in a horror attraction.

So I did my research in bursts. A few minutes here and there between client calls, longer sessions during lunch breaks, late-night deep dives when I couldn't sleep.

"You're distracted," Julie said during our Wednesday check-in call.

I forced myself to focus on the screen, where she was presenting the latest round of temp placements. She was right—I'd been half-listening, my mind wandering to the interview I'd read that morning where Wylder talked about his "immersive psychological experiences."

"Sorry, just tired. Late night last night." Not entirely a lie. I'd been up until two researching the building Wylder had leased. "The law firm placement looks good. Send over the contracts."

"Actually, they want to amend their original request. They need three more paralegals now."

"Even better. Barb has applications coming out her ears."

After we hung up, I made myself a fresh cup of coffee and tried to focus on actual work. The temp agency was booming—we had more placements than ever, three new corporate contracts in the pipeline, and a waiting list of qualified candidates. But even as I worked on staffing schedules and client proposals, part of my brain kept circling back to Wylder.

"Britney?" Barb knocked on my office door, holding a stack of pink message slips. "You've got about ten callbacks, and that new medical practice wants to schedule an interview for their front desk position."

I waved her in. "Anything urgent?"

She flipped through the messages. "Ben Peterson called. Says he's swamped again and needs two more temp receptionists if we have them."

I smiled. Ben kept our lights on with his constant need for temporary staff. His practice had exploded over the past year. "Call Sarah Martinez and Lisa Chen. They're both available for immediate placement."

"On it." Barb paused. "Also, there's someone here for an interview. Says she doesn't have an appointment but she's desperate."

I glanced at my calendar. I had twenty minutes before my next client call. "Send her back."

But even as I worked on staffing schedules and client proposals, part of my brain kept circling back to what I'd learned. Wylder wasn't just some amateur trying to cash in on the horror trend. He'd spent two years developing Nightmares Unleashed, working with psychologists and trauma specialists to create what he called "therapeutic terror."

The more I read, the angrier I got. He was taking people's worst experiences—abuse, manipulation, psychological torture—and turning them into entertainment. Worse, he claimed it would help people heal.

I knew what healing looked like. It was messy and painful and took years of work with someone like Ben. It wasn't something you could package into a two-hour experience and charge admission for.

Around lunch, Barb stuck her head in my office. "Coffee run. Want anything?"

"Please. I'm going to dream of spreadsheets if I don't get more caffeine."

She laughed. "The usual?"

"Extra shot today."

While she was gone, I allowed myself a quick research session. James Wylder had done another interview, this one with a local podcaster who specialized in "alternative healing methods." I put my earbuds in and listened while sorting through applications.

The more Wylder talked, the more I wanted to reach through the screen and throttle him. He kept using words like "breakthrough" and "revolutionary" and "cathartic therapy." Like he'd invented some new form of healing instead of just repackaging trauma for profit.

My phone buzzed with a text from Stu: *Working late tonight. Chinese food?*

I glanced at the clock—4:30. Good thing I was wrapping up for the day anyway. The traffic was going to be awful enough even if I left earlier.

Sure. Usual order.

Love you.

Love you too.

I finished up the last few applications and started shutting down for the day. Barb was packing up at her desk, and Julie had already left for the day. We kept strict business hours at the agency—no late nights, no weekend work unless it was an absolute emergency.

I locked up the office and headed home, cursing Tampa traffic the entire way. Twenty minutes in stop-and-go hell just to travel what should have been a ten-minute drive. By the time I finally pulled into the driveway, I was ready to feed Minion and collapse. She was already sitting by her bowl, giving me that judgmental look cats had perfected.

"Yeah, yeah, I'm late," I muttered, opening a can of the expensive food she preferred. "Sue me."

She headbutted my leg in forgiveness once the food hit her bowl, and I scratched behind her ears while she ate. These quiet moments with her were some of the few times my brain actually stopped spinning.

But not for long. While I waited for Stu to get home with dinner, I found myself back on my laptop, this time looking at local news coverage of Nightmares Unleashed.

The preview event was generating serious buzz. The reporter described it as "the most ambitious horror attraction to hit the area," and mentioned that tickets were "extremely limited" and expected to sell out within minutes of going on sale.

Limited tickets meant I'd have to move fast when they became available. It also meant Wylder was creating artificial scarcity to build hype. Classic marketing move, and one I'd used myself for clients.

I dug deeper into the event details. The preview was invitation-only for media, local influencers, and what Wylder called "horror enthusiasts." The public sale wouldn't happen until after the preview, assuming it went well.

That complicated things. I wasn't media, definitely wasn't an influencer, and I doubted my true level of horror enthusiasm was what Wylder had in mind.

But there had to be a way in. There always was.

I was still researching when Stu got home, the smell of Chinese food filling the house.

"How was your day?" he asked, setting the bags on the kitchen table.

"Productive," I said, closing the laptop. "Yours?"

"Same old shit. Though I did have to break up a domestic dispute call." He paused, giving me a look I couldn't quite read. "Reminded me why I hate those."

I knew that look. It was the same one he'd gotten when I told him about Dario, about what I'd endured before I finally learned to fight back.

"Bad?"

"Bad enough. Woman had a black eye, claimed she fell down stairs. Guy wouldn't stop talking, trying to explain why it wasn't his fault, why she was asking for it." Stu's jaw tightened. "Made me want to do things that would get me fired."

I reached over and took his hand. "But you didn't."

"No. But I wanted to."

We ate in comfortable silence for a while, both lost in our own thoughts. It wasn't until we were cleaning up that Stu brought up what I'd been hoping he wouldn't notice.

"You've been on that laptop a lot lately. Still researching our friend?"

"James Wylder. And yeah." I rinsed the plates and handed them to him to dry. "The more I learn about him, the more I want to make him disappear."

"What'd you find out?"

I told him about the preview event, about the limited access and artificial scarcity. About the interviews where Wylder positioned himself as some kind of trauma therapy pioneer.

"Guy sounds like a real piece of work," Stu said.

"He's worse than that. He's dangerous. Not in the obvious way—he's not out there hurting people directly. But what he's doing. . . it's going to mess people up. People who are already struggling, who think maybe this could actually help them."

Stu nodded, understanding exactly what I meant. "So what's the plan?"

"First, I need to get into that preview event. See what he's actually created."

"And then?"

I smiled, feeling that familiar warmth. "Then I show him what real terror looks like."

Later that night, Stu and I settled on the couch to watch a movie. We needed something mindless to help us both unwind—him from that domestic violence call he'd mentioned, me from my growing obsession with Wylder.

"What are you in the mood for?" he asked, scrolling through Netflix.

"Nothing that requires thinking," I said, letting Minion claim her usual spot between us. "Comedy? Action? I don't care as long as no one gets psychologically tortured."

Stu gave me a look. "That bad, huh?"

"Getting there."

He settled on some ridiculous action movie with explosions and one-liners. Perfect. For two hours, I managed to focus on something other than James Wylder and his sick little project.

But as the credits rolled and we headed upstairs, my mind was already spinning again. Tomorrow I'd have to dive deeper into researching the preview event, figure out how to get an invitation. This kind of planning took time—days, maybe weeks of careful research and preparation.

I wasn't going to rush it. Not when the payoff would be so satisfying.

The next morning brought another text from an unknown number: *Getting excited for next week? I know I am. —Your friend J*

I stared at the message over my morning coffee, ice cubes melting slowly. The fact that he was still contacting me, still playing whatever game this was, told me everything I needed to know about his personality.

He was a control freak who couldn't resist push-ing boundaries. He thought he was the one calling the shots, the one with the power.

He was about to learn how wrong he was.

I screenshot the message and sent it to Stu, then blocked the number. If Wylder wanted to play games, he could do it with someone else. I had work to do.

But first, I had to get through another day of pretending to care about temp placements and client needs. The mask was getting heavier, but I'd worn it for years. I could manage a few more days.

At least until I could show James Wylder what happened to people who turned other people's pain into profit.

I finished my coffee and opened my laptop, forcing myself to focus on work. But in the back of my mind, I was already planning.

Three

Friday morning started like any other day at the office, except I had a plan forming. Getting into that preview event wasn't going to be as simple as buying a ticket—it was invitation-only, which meant I needed to become someone worth inviting.

"Morning, Britney," Barb called as I walked through the front door. She was already at her desk, sorting through applications. "Coffee's fresh."

"You're a saint." I grabbed my usual mug and added three ice cubes. "What's on the schedule today?"

"Light day. Julie's got two client meetings this afternoon, and Ben Peterson called about extending his temp contracts through the end of the month."

I nodded, settling into my office. Ben's steady business was one of the things that kept us profitable—his therapy practice had exploded over the past year, probably because he was so good at what he did. I should know, considering he was my therapist too. But today I was more interested in the stack of local business magazines Barb had left on my desk. I'd asked her to grab anything that mentioned the Tampa Bay area's entertainment or business scene.

I flipped through the first magazine, looking for any mention of Nightmares Unleashed or James Wylder. Nothing. The second one had a small blurb about "upcoming attractions," but it was just the basic information I already knew.

Then I hit gold in the third magazine—a full-page interview with Wylder titled "Local Entrepreneur Brings Fear to Life." The photo showed him standing in front of construction barriers, hard hat in hand, looking like the confident businessman he thought he was.

"Horror has always been about exploring the human psyche," Wylder explained during our interview. "But most attractions focus on cheap thrills. What we're creating at Nightmares Unleashed is something deeper—a chance for people to confront their fears in a controlled environment and emerge stronger."

I had to stop reading before I grabbed my lighter and set the magazine on fire. This asshole really believed his own bullshit.

But the interview gave me what I needed. At the bottom, there was a mention of a "select group of local business leaders and influencers" who would be attending the preview event. The magazine didn't list names, but it gave me a direction.

I needed to become one of those local business leaders.

My phone rang, interrupting my planning. "Passing Through, Britney speaking."

"Britney! Thank God you answered." It was Marcus Chen, one of our biggest corporate clients. "I've got an emergency. Our entire reception staff just quit—something about hostile work environment—and we've got board meetings all next week."

I smiled. This was exactly the kind of crisis that had built my reputation. "How many people do you need?"

"Three, maybe four. Professional, can handle high-pressure situations. These board members can be. . . demanding."

"I've got the perfect people. When do you need them?"

"Monday morning. Is that possible?"

"Marcus, it's me. Of course it's possible." I was already mentally going through my available temps. "I'll have them there at eight sharp, fully briefed and ready to handle whatever your board throws at them."

"You're a lifesaver. Send me the contracts and I'll get them signed today."

After I hung up, I called Julie to handle the placement details, then turned my attention back to my real problem. How does a temp agency owner become influential enough to get invited to an exclusive preview event?

The answer came to me while I was reviewing our quarterly numbers. Passing Through had grown significantly over the past year. We were now the largest temp agency in the Tampa Bay area, with contracts at major corporations, law firms, medical practices, and even city government offices.

On paper, I was already a local business leader. I just needed to make sure the right people knew it.

I spent the next hour crafting an email to the Tampa Bay Business Journal. I pitched them a story about the growth of the temporary staffing industry, positioning myself as an expert on local employment trends. It was the kind of dry business content they loved, and it would get my name in front of their readership—which included people like James Wylder.

By lunch, I'd sent similar pitches to three other local publications and started following several Tampa business networking groups on social media. I even updated my LinkedIn profile to emphasize my role in the local business community.

It was all groundwork. The kind of slow, methodical building that would pay off when I needed it to.

"Working through lunch again?" Barb asked, appearing in my doorway with a bag from Moxie's.

"You didn't have to—"

"Turkey melt, no tomato, extra cheese." She set it on my desk. "You've been distracted all week. Everything okay?"

I looked up at her, this woman who'd been with me since almost the beginning. Barb was smart, observant, and loyal. She'd seen me through enough moods to know when something was off.

"Just thinking about expanding our marketing," I said, which wasn't entirely a lie. "Trying to raise our profile in the business community."

"Good idea. We've got the track record for it." She hesitated. "You sure that's all it is?"

"What do you mean?"

"You've been. . . intense lately. More than usual. And you keep checking your phone like you're waiting for something."

I forced myself to smile. "Just excited about some new opportunities. Nothing to worry about."

Barb didn't look convinced, but she nodded. "Okay. But if you need to talk, you know I'm here."

After she left, I sat back in my chair and tried to see myself through her eyes. Was I being that obvious? I'd have to be more careful. The last thing I needed was Barb getting suspicious right when I was planning something this complicated.

I ate my melt and got back to work, forcing myself to focus on legitimate business for the rest of the afternoon. I reviewed Julie's client proposals, approved three new temp placements, and even took a call from a potential new corporate client.

But in the back of my mind, I was calculating. The preview event was next Friday—eight days away. That gave me just over a week to establish myself as someone worth inviting.

It wasn't much time, but it might be enough.

When I got home that evening, Stu was already there, sitting at the kitchen table with a beer and a stack of paperwork.

"Rough day?" I asked, kissing the top of his head.

"Just paperwork. You?"

"Productive." I grabbed a glass of wine and sat across from him. "I think I figured out how to get into that preview event."

Stu looked up from his reports. "How?"

I explained my plan—the media outreach, the business networking, the attempt to position myself as a local business leader worth inviting.

"That's. . . smart," he said when I finished. "But will it work in just over a week?"

"It has to." I took a sip of wine. "The alternative is trying to sneak in, and that's too risky. This way, I get invited legitimately. No one questions why I'm there."

"And after you see what he's built?"

"Then I start planning the real fun." I smiled. "But first, I need to see what I'm working with. Know your enemy and all that."

Stu nodded, understanding. We'd been through this dance before—the careful planning, the patient observation, the methodical approach. It was one of the things I loved about him. He got the process.

"Anything I can do to help?"

"Just keep being my alibi," I said. "When the time comes, I'll need you to provide cover."

"Always."

We finished dinner and settled on the couch to watch something goofy on TV. But I was only half-paying attention. My mind was running through contingencies, backup plans, ways to make sure my networking gambit worked.

James Wylder thought he was so clever, creating controlled fear for paying customers. He had no idea what real fear looked like. But he would.

The next morning brought good news. The Tampa Bay Business Journal had responded to my pitch, asking for more details about my story idea. They were interested in running a piece about the temp industry's growth, with me as the primary source.

I spent Saturday morning putting together a detailed proposal, complete with statistics about job growth, economic impact, and the changing nature of work in the Tampa Bay area. It was the kind of data-driven story business publications loved.

By Monday, I had confirmation. They wanted to schedule an interview for Wednesday, with the article running in Friday's issue—the same day as the preview event.

Good timing.

Tuesday, I got another break. The Tampa Chamber of Commerce called, asking if I'd be interested in speaking at their next quarterly meeting about entrepreneurship and job creation. I said yes immediately.

Wednesday's interview went as planned. The journalist was young, eager, and completely bought into my narrative about being a local business success story. She asked all the right questions, and I gave all the right answers.

"You're really impressive," she said as we wrapped up. "I had no idea the temp industry was such a big part of the local economy."

"Most people don't," I replied. "We're usually behind the scenes, keeping other businesses running."

"Well, this article should help change that. It'll be in Friday's issue, both print and online."

That evening, I allowed myself a small celebration. One glass of wine, shared with Stu while Minion purred between us on the couch.

"Think it'll work?" he asked.

"It has to," I said. "I've done everything short of taking out a billboard advertising my business credentials."

"And if Wylder doesn't bite?"

I smiled. "Then I get creative. But something tells me he will. Men like him love being around other successful people. Makes them feel important."

Thursday crawled by. I kept checking my email, my phone, the Nightmares Unleashed website, looking for any sign that my plan was working.

Nothing.

Friday morning, the Business Journal article went live. "Local Entrepreneur Builds Empire One Temp at a Time" ran both in print and online, complete with a professional photo of me in my office.

I'd barely finished my morning coffee when my phone rang.

Unknown number.

"Britney Cage."

"Ms. Cage, this is Jennifer Walsh, assistant to James Wylder. I'm calling about tonight's preview event for Nightmares Unleashed."

My heart rate spiked, but I kept my voice calm. "Oh?"

"Mr. Wylder read your article in the Business Journal this morning and was very impressed with your business acumen. He'd like to extend an invitation to tonight's preview, if you're available."

"Tonight?" I paused, as if checking my calendar. "You know what, I think I can make it work. What time?"

"Seven PM for the preview experience, followed by a cocktail reception at nine. The address is 4247 Industrial Boulevard. There will be valet parking and hors d'oeuvres."

"Sounds lovely. Should I bring anything?"

"Just yourself. Oh, and feel free to bring a guest if you'd like."

I thought about Stu. For this kind of reconnaissance, I'd need his eyes too. He saw things differently than I did, noticed details I might miss. And when it came to reading people—especially dangerous people—having another psychopath's perspective would be valuable.

"Actually, I'd love to bring my fiancé, if that's all right."

"Of course. Mr. Wylder is looking forward to meeting you both."

After I hung up, I sat back in my chair and smiled. Phase one was complete.

Tonight, I'd get my first look at James Wylder's sick little fantasy world. And Stu would be there to watch him with me, to catch the things I might miss.

Two predators observing their prey.

And then the real planning could begin.

Four

STU AND I ARRIVED at Nightmares Unleashed at seven sharp. The building looked like something out of a horror movie itself—an old industrial warehouse painted matte black, with minimal lighting that made the shadows seem to move. Valet attendants in crisp black uniforms took our keys, and I noticed they were all young, attractive, and looked like they'd been cast for the role.

"Nice touch," Stu murmured as we walked toward the entrance. "Sets the mood."

The front doors were heavy steel painted to look rusted and weathered. Above them, "Nightmares Unleashed" glowed in red neon, the letters designed to look like they were dripping blood.

Inside, the lobby was all black marble and dim lighting. About thirty people milled around, champagne glasses in hand, looking like the local business elite I'd expected. I recognized a few faces from the Business Journal's social pages—real estate developers, restaurant owners, a city councilman.

"Ms. Cage!" A woman in an expensive black suit approached us with a clipboard. "I'm Jennifer Walsh, we spoke on the phone. So glad you could make it."

"Wouldn't miss it," I replied, shaking her hand. "This is my fiancé, Stu Jones."

"Wonderful to meet you both. Mr. Wylder is just finishing up with another guest, but he's very eager to meet you. Can I get you something to drink?"

We accepted glasses of champagne and made small talk with Jennifer about the turnout, the venue, the excitement around the project. She was good at her job—professional, enthusiastic, but not pushy. I could see why Wylder had hired her.

"Britney Cage!"

I turned to see a man approaching us with the kind of confident stride that screamed "I own this room." James Wylder was what I'd expected from his photos—early fifties, salt-and-pepper hair perfectly styled, expensive suit that fit like it was tailored for him. He stood about six feet tall with a slightly burly build that suggested he'd been athletic in his younger days. Despite the predatory confidence in his walk, he had the kind of broad shoulders and thick arms that looked like he'd give bear hugs. The contradiction was unsettling—someone who could appear warm and safe while being anything but. He had the look of someone who'd never been told no.

"Mr. Wylder," I said, extending my hand. "Thank you so much for the invitation."

His handshake was firm, lingering just a second too long. "Please, call me James. And you must be the fiancé—Stu, right?"

"That's right," Stu replied, his own handshake brief and professional.

James's eyes lingered on Stu for a moment, and I could see him sizing up the competition. Stu was younger, taller, and had the kind of quiet confidence that didn't need to announce itself. I watched James's smile tighten.

"I have to say, Britney, that article about you in the Business Journal was fascinating. The temp industry doesn't usually get that kind of spotlight."

"Most people don't realize how integral we are to the local economy," I responded. "Every major business in the area has used our services at some point."

"Including mine, actually. We hired several of your people during the construction phase." James gestured around the lobby. "Outstanding work ethic. Very professional."

I smiled. "I remember that contract. Industrial construction cleanup, if I recall correctly."

"Exactly. Which is why I was so interested to meet you in person." James moved closer, lowering his voice slightly. "Someone with your business acumen would really appreciate what we're trying to accomplish here."

"I'm intrigued," I said, letting just enough interest creep into my voice.

"Traditional horror attractions are so. . . simplistic. Jump scares, fake blood, actors in rubber masks. It's entertainment for teenagers." James's voice took on the passionate tone I'd heard in his interviews. "What we've created here is psychological horror. Real fear, carefully controlled and channeled into something transformative."

"Transformative how?" Stu asked.

James turned to him, and I caught a flash of annoyance that he'd been interrupted. "Fear is one of our most primal emotions. When we face it head-on, when we survive it, we become stronger. More resilient. The experience here isn't just entertainment—it's therapy."

I had to work to keep my expression neutral. This close to him, listening to him talk about trauma and fear like he was some kind of expert, I could feel my anger building. But I needed to play the part.

"That's a fascinating approach," I said. "How did you develop the concept?"

"Years of research," James replied, his chest puffing slightly with pride. "I worked with therapists, trauma specialists, even spent time studying PTSD treatment protocols. The goal was to create controlled fear scenarios that mirror real psychological triggers, but in a safe environment where people can process and overcome them."

"And you've tested this approach?" Stu's question had just enough skepticism to sound natural.

"Extensively. We had focus groups, beta testing with volunteers. The feedback has been positive." James paused, studying Stu more carefully. "What do you do for work, if you don't mind me asking?"

"Law enforcement," Stu replied simply.

"Ah." James's expression shifted slightly. "Then you understand trauma. You've probably seen how it affects people."

"I have."

"Then you'll appreciate what we're doing here. Police officers, first responders, military personnel—you're some of the people who could benefit most from this kind of therapeutic experience."

I watched Stu's expression harden. "How so?"

"Controlled exposure to fear and stress, in an environment where you know you're safe. It can help process traumatic experiences, build resilience, even treat symptoms of PTSD." James was warming to his subject. "Imagine being able to face your worst fears and walk away stronger."

"Interesting theory," Stu said in a tone that suggested it was anything but.

James either didn't catch the sarcasm or chose to ignore it. "The beauty of what we've created is the customization. Each experience is tailored to the individual's specific fears and triggers. We have intake questionnaires, psychological profiles—"

"You profile your customers?" I interrupted.

"Not in a clinical sense," James said quickly. "But we do gather information about what scares them most. Claustrophobia, abandonment, betrayal, loss of control—everyone has different triggers. The more we know, the more effective the experience becomes."

I felt a chill that had nothing to do with fear. James Wylder wasn't just exploiting people's trauma for entertainment—he was collecting their deepest vulnerabilities like trophies.

"That level of personalization must require significant resources," I said.

"It does. We have a full psychological staff, plus actors trained in method techniques. Every scenario is carefully scripted and monitored." James gestured toward a hallway that led deeper into the building. "Would you like a preview of what we've built? I'd love to show you some of the technology we're using."

I glanced at Stu, who gave an almost imperceptible nod.

"We'd love to see it," I said.

James led us down a dimly lit corridor lined with what looked like dressing room doors. "Each of these rooms is a different scenario," he explained. "Domestic violence, workplace harassment, childhood trauma, medical emergencies—we've built complete environments for dozens of different fear categories."

He stopped in front of one door and produced a key card. "This is one of our most popular scenarios. Mind if I show you?"

The door opened onto what looked like a normal living room—couch, coffee table, family photos on the walls. But something about it felt wrong. The lighting was too harsh, the furniture positioned in a way that created shadows and blind spots.

"Domestic abuse scenario," James said matter-of-factly. "The participant enters thinking they're safe, but then the environment slowly becomes more threatening. Sound effects, lighting changes, carefully placed triggers that recreate the psychological dynamics of an abusive relationship."

I stared at the room, fighting the urge to grab James by the throat. He was talking about recreating domestic violence like it was a theme park ride.

"The goal is to help survivors process their experiences in a controlled setting," he continued. "Face their fears, reclaim their power."

"And if they're not survivors?" Stu asked. "If they're just tourists looking for thrills?"

James shrugged. "Then they get a very intense education about what real trauma looks like. Either way, they leave changed."

"Changed how?" I managed to ask.

"Stronger. More empathetic. Better equipped to handle real crisis situations." James closed the door and turned back to us. "That's the beauty of therapeutic horror—it doesn't just entertain, it transforms."

We continued down the hallway as James showed us glimpses of other scenarios. A hospital room designed to trigger medical trauma. An office setup that recreated workplace harassment. A bedroom that looked innocent until you noticed the hidden cameras and locks on the windows.

Each room made my skin crawl more than the last. This wasn't therapy—it was psychological torture disguised as entertainment.

"The technology integration is what sets us apart," James said as we walked. "Biometric monitoring, real-time psychological assessment, adaptive scenario progression. We can watch someone's fear response and adjust the experience accordingly."

"You monitor their physical responses?" Stu asked.

"Heart rate, perspiration, stress hormones—we track everything. It helps us calibrate the intensity and know when to dial things back for safety."

"Or when to push harder for maximum impact," I said.

James smiled. "Exactly. You really do understand business psychology."

We reached the end of the hallway, where James stopped in front of a heavy door marked "Control Room."

"This is where the magic happens," he said, using his key card again. "Our central monitoring station."

The control room looked like something from a high-end security company. Banks of monitors showed feeds from every scenario room, with real-time data streaming across screens showing heart rates, stress levels, and other biometric information.

"We can monitor up to fifty participants at once," James said proudly. "Full audio and video, plus all the biometric data. If someone's genuinely in distress, we can intervene immediately."

"How do you tell the difference between genuine distress and the fear response you're trying to create?" I asked.

"Experience. Training. And sophisticated monitoring software." James gestured to one of the technicians. "Our staff includes licensed therapists and medical professionals. Safety is our top priority."

I doubted that. From what I'd seen, profit was his top priority, with sadism running a close second.

"How long do the experiences typically last?" Stu asked.

"Anywhere from thirty minutes to two hours, depending on the scenario and the participant's response. Some people break through their fears quickly. Others need more time to process."

"And if they want to stop?"

"Safe words, panic buttons, multiple exit points. We're careful about consent." James paused. "Though I will say, many people think they want to quit when they're on the verge of a break-through. That's where our psychological staff earns their money."

Translation: they talk people out of leaving when they should. I was starting to understand how James operated—push boundaries, ignore comfort zones, and convince people it was for their own good. Classic abuser tactics dressed up as therapy.

"Well," James said, checking his watch, "we should head back. The preview experience starts in about ten minutes."

As we walked back toward the lobby, James continued his sales pitch. "I think you'd both benefit from the full experience. Britney, we have scenarios designed for high-achieving professionals dealing with control issues and perfectionism. And Stu, our first responder protocols are effective."

"Control issues?" I asked.

"Successful business owners often struggle with delegation, trust, fear of failure. Our scenarios help you confront those fears in a safe space." James's smile had a predatory edge. "I'd be interested to see how you respond to a scenario where you're completely powerless."

The irony was lost on him. James Wylder had no idea that he was talking to someone who understood powerlessness—and who'd made a career of taking power away from people like him.

"That does sound intriguing," I said. "What exactly would that involve?"

"I'd rather not spoil the surprise. But I will say our intake process is thorough. We'd want to understand your specific fears and triggers before designing your experience."

"Of course."

We reached the lobby, where the other guests were being organized into groups. Jennifer appeared with another clipboard, looking efficient and professional.

"Ladies and gentlemen, if I could have your attention," she announced. "We're ready to begin tonight's preview experience. You'll be divided into groups of six for tonight's journey."

James placed a hand on my arm. "I've arranged for you and Stu to be in the first group. VIP treatment for VIP guests."

"You're too kind," I replied.

As we joined the other four people in our group, James leaned closer. "After the experience, I'd love to continue our conversation at the cocktail reception. I have a feeling we have a lot to discuss."

"I'm looking forward to it," I said.

And I was. Not for the reasons James thought, but because every minute I spent with him gave me more insight into how his mind worked. By the time

I was done with him, James Wylder would understand exactly what powerlessness felt like.

But first, I needed to see what he'd built. I needed to experience his version of controlled fear so I could show him what the uncontrolled version looked like.

Five

"LADIES AND GENTLEMEN, IF you could follow me," Jennifer said, leading our group of six toward a set of double doors marked "Experience Entrance." "Before we begin, I need to collect your phones and any other electronic devices. They'll be returned after the experience."

I reluctantly handed over my phone, watching as the others did the same. A young man who looked like he worked in tech seemed particularly anxious about being separated from his device.

"Now, you'll each be fitted with a monitoring bracelet," Jennifer continued, pulling out a tray of what looked like fitness trackers. "These monitor your heart rate and stress levels for safety purposes. If your readings become dangerous, we can intervene immediately."

The bracelet felt heavier than it looked, and I noticed a small green light that blinked steadily once it was secured around my wrist. They were watching us.

"The experience is customized based on the intake questionnaires you filled out earlier," Jennifer explained as she led us down another corridor. "Each of you will face scenarios designed specifically for your psychological profile."

I hadn't filled out any questionnaire, but I kept my mouth shut. Being a VIP guest meant skipping some of the preparation.

We stopped in front of six doors, each marked with a number. "You'll be entering individual experiences," Jennifer said. "The scenarios are designed to be completed alone, as isolation intensifies the psychological impact."

My stomach dropped. I'd been counting on having Stu with me, on having someone I trusted watching my back. But I couldn't object without seeming suspicious.

"How long does each experience last?" Asked a woman in her forties who'd introduced herself as a real estate developer.

"It varies based on your responses and how quickly you progress through the scenarios. Anywhere from forty-five minutes to two hours." Jennifer smiled. "Don't worry, you're safe. We're monitoring everything."

That was supposed to be reassuring, but it wasn't. The idea of James Wylder and his staff watching my every reaction, cataloging my fears, made my skin crawl.

"Britney, you'll be in Room 3," Jennifer said, handing me a key card. "Just follow the instructions on the screen when you enter. Remember, this is about facing your fears and emerging stronger."

I looked at Stu, trying to communicate my unease without words. He gave me a barely perceptible nod—he understood. But there was nothing either of us could do without blowing our cover.

"See you on the other side," he said quietly as Jennifer led him toward Room 5.

I swiped the key card and stepped into Room 3, hearing the door lock behind me with a definitive click.

The room was small and white, like a medical examination room. A single chair sat in the center, facing a large monitor mounted on the wall. Text appeared on the screen:

Welcome, Britney. Please take a seat and we'll begin your personalized experience. Remember, everything you're about to encounter is designed to help you grow. Trust the process.

I sat down, hyperaware of the monitoring bracelet on my wrist. The green light was blinking faster.

Based on your psychological profile as a successful business owner, we've designed an experience focused on control, trust, and vulnerability. You will be placed in situations where your usual coping mechanisms won't work. This is intentional.

The screen went black, and suddenly the lights dimmed to almost nothing. I could barely see the chair I was sitting in.

A voice came from speakers hidden in the walls—warm, professional, female. "Hello, Britney. My name is Dr. Sarah, and I'll be guiding you through today's experience. I want you to know that you're safe, but for the next hour, you won't be in control. Are you ready to begin?"

Every instinct I had was screaming at me to get up and leave. But I needed to see what James had built, needed to understand how he operated.

"I'm ready," I said to the darkness.

"Good. In a moment, you're going to feel some mild disorientation. This is normal. Just breathe and trust the process."

I felt something change in the air—a subtle shift in pressure, maybe some kind of gas being pumped in. Nothing dangerous, just enough to make me feel off-balance.

"Very good. Your heart rate has increased, but you're managing well. Now, I want you to stand up and walk toward the wall directly in front of you."

I stood, reaching out with my hands to navigate in the darkness. When I touched the wall, a section of it slid away, revealing a narrow corridor lit by flickering fluorescent lights.

"Walk forward, Britney. Don't look back."

The corridor was longer than it seemed at first, and the flickering lights created disorienting shadows. I could hear sounds coming from other rooms—muffled voices, sometimes crying, occasionally what sounded like screaming. My bracelet was blinking rapidly.

"You're doing well," Dr. Sarah's voice followed me through speakers mounted in the ceiling. "How are you feeling right now?"

"Fine," I lied.

"Your biometrics suggest otherwise. Elevated heart rate, increased perspiration, muscle tension. It's okay to admit you're afraid."

I didn't respond. The corridor ended at another door, which opened automatically as I approached.

The next room was a replica of an office—desk, computer, filing cabinets, even a coffee maker. But something was wrong with it. The proportions were off, making everything feel cramped and claustrophobic.

"This is your office, Britney. Or rather, it was. Please, sit at the desk."

I moved to the chair, noting that it was positioned so I couldn't see the door I'd entered through. The computer screen came to life, showing what looked like email messages.

"Read the first email," Dr. Sarah instructed.

From: Florida Department of Labor To: Britney Cage Subject: Business License Revocation

Ms. Cage, Due to recent violations of state employment law and multiple complaints filed against Passing Through Temp Agency, your business license is revoked effective immediately. All opera-

tions must cease. You are prohibited from operating any staffing business in the state of Florida.

My rational mind knew this was fake, part of the experience. But something about seeing it on a screen, in an office that looked so much like mine, made my chest tighten.

"How does that make you feel?" Dr. Sarah asked.

"It's not real," I said.

"But if it were? If everything you'd built was taken away in an instant? If you had no control over your own fate?"

The screen changed, showing what looked like financial records. Numbers in red, accounts being drained, everything I'd worked for disappearing.

"Your heart rate is spiking, Britney. This is good—you're engaging with the experience. Now, I want you to try to leave the room."

I stood and turned toward where the door had been, but the wall was solid. I ran my hands along the surface, looking for a seam or a handle. Nothing.

"There's no way out right now," Dr. Sarah said. "You're completely dependent on me to guide you through this. How does that feel?"

I didn't answer, but I could feel my breathing getting shallower. The room seemed to be getting smaller, the walls closing in. I knew it was an illusion, probably just the lighting changing, but knowing didn't make it less effective.

"Let's try a different scenario," Dr. Sarah continued. "You're being investigated. The police are involved. Your reputation is destroyed."

The computer screen changed again, showing what looked like news articles with my photo. Headlines about fraud, embezzlement, criminal charges. None of it was real, but the effect was visceral.

"Everyone you trusted has turned against you. Your employees, your clients, even your fiancé. You're completely alone."

The screen showed text messages, supposedly from Stu. *I can't do this anymore. I'm leaving. Don't try to contact me.*

I knew it was fake. I knew Stu would never send messages like that. But trapped in this room, isolated and monitored, part of my brain started to believe it.

"Your stress levels are high," Dr. Sarah observed. "But you're still fighting the experience. That's common with people who are used to being in control. Let's see if we can break through that resistance."

The lights went out, plunging me into absolute darkness. I could hear my own breathing, magnified somehow, and the sound of my heart beating through the bracelet's monitoring system.

"You're going to hear some sounds now, Britney. Try not to let them disturb you."

First came the sound of footsteps in the corridor outside—slow, deliberate, getting closer. Then voices, low and threatening, though I couldn't make out the words. The sounds seemed to be coming from all around me, even though I knew they were from speakers.

"Someone's coming for you," Dr. Sarah whispered. "Someone who knows what you've done. There's nowhere to run."

I pressed myself against the wall, trying to stay calm. This was psychological manipulation, nothing more. But the darkness, the isolation, the constant monitoring—it was working. I could feel my control slipping.

The sounds got louder. Footsteps, voices, what sounded like doors slamming. My bracelet was blinking so fast it was almost solid light.

"Please," I found myself saying. "I want to stop."

"The safe word is 'mercy,'" Dr. Sarah said. "But are you sure you want to quit? You're so close to a breakthrough. This is where real growth happens."

I thought about James Wylder watching all of this, studying my reactions, getting off on my fear. The idea made me angry enough to push through the panic.

"I'm not saying the safe word," I said through gritted teeth.

"Good. Then let's continue."

A door opened—not the one I'd come through, but a new one I hadn't noticed before. Light spilled in from the next room, and I could see stairs leading down.

"Go down the stairs, Britney. Face what's waiting for you in the basement."

Every horror movie I'd ever seen told me not to go into the basement. But I needed to see this through, needed to understand the full scope of what James had created.

The stairs were steep and narrow, and I had to use the handrail to keep from falling. At the bottom was another room, this one designed to look like a basement workshop. Tools hung from pegboards, workbenches lined the walls, and the lighting was dim and yellow.

But it was the smell that got to me—chemicals, disinfectant, and something else I couldn't identify but that made my stomach turn.

"This is where it ends," Dr. Sarah said, her voice different now. Colder. "This is where people like you come when their control runs out."

On one of the workbenches, I could see what looked like restraints. Rope, handcuffs, zip ties. My mind flashed to all the true crime documentaries I'd watched, all the stories of people who'd disappeared, every horror movie basement scene that ended badly.

"Your bracelet shows you're experiencing genuine terror," Dr. Sarah observed. "Your stress hormones are flooding your system. This is what we want—pure, primal fear with nowhere to run."

I backed toward the stairs, but I could hear them retracting behind me, becoming smooth wall.

"There's no going back, Britney. Only forward."

A figure stepped out of the shadows—a man in coveralls and a mask, carrying what looked like a length of rope. I knew it was an actor, knew this was all fake, but my body didn't care. I felt genuine terror for the first time in years.

The figure moved closer, and I could hear his breathing through the mask. Heavy, deliberate. He set the rope down on the workbench and picked up something else—pliers, the metal gleaming under the yellow lights.

"Your stress levels are off the charts," Dr. Sarah whispered. "This is perfect. You're experiencing pure, unfiltered fear."

The masked figure approached me slowly, methodically, like he had all the time in the world. I pressed myself against the wall, but there was nowhere to go. He reached out with the pliers, bringing them close to my face.

"The beauty of our monitoring system," Dr. Sarah continued, "is that we know how far we can push you. Your body is flooded with adrenaline, but you're not in actual danger. We can take you right to the edge."

The pliers touched my cheek, cold metal against skin. I could smell something sharp and chemical, like cleaning supplies mixed with something organic and rotten. The figure's breathing grew heavier.

"Some of our clients pay extra for this level of intensity," Dr. Sarah said. "The complete power-lessness experience. You should feel honored."

The figure grabbed my wrist—not the one with the monitoring bracelet—and examined my hand with disturbing interest. The pliers hovered over my fingers.

I wanted to fight back, wanted to show this asshole what real violence looked like. But I was trapped in his scenario, playing by his rules. For now.

"Perfect fear response," Dr. Sarah murmured. "James is going to be very pleased with tonight's data."

The lights went out again, plunging us back into darkness. I could hear the figure moving around me, circling, the sound of metal tools clinking to-gether on the workbench.

"Time for the final test," Dr. Sarah whispered.

Six

I PRESSED MYSELF HARDER against the wall, trying to become invisible. The sound of footsteps stopped directly in front of me. I could feel his presence, smell his sweat mixed with something metallic.

"Your heart rate is at dangerous levels," Dr. Sarah observed. "But that's what makes this so effective. The body doesn't know the difference between real and simulated terror."

A hand grabbed my shoulder, fingers digging in hard enough to bruise. I jerked away, but there was nowhere to go. The figure's breathing was getting heavier, more excited.

"Most people break by now," Dr. Sarah continued. "They beg, they cry, they use the safe word. But you're still fighting. That's admirable. And profitable."

Profitable? What the hell did that mean?

The figure dragged me away from the wall toward what I assumed was the workbench. I could hear more tools being moved around, metal scraping against metal. Something that sounded like a drill whirring to life.

"The beauty of our system," Dr. Sarah said, "is that we can simulate any experience. Kidnapping, torture, murder—all the fears that keep people awake at night. And we can make it feel completely real."

The drill sound got closer. I could feel the vibration against my arm, though it wasn't actually touching me. The psychological effect was the same—pure, primal terror.

"Some clients pay extra for the full experience," Dr. Sarah whispered. "Complete helplessness. Complete surrender. They want to know what it feels like to face death and survive."

I felt restraints being wrapped around my wrists—not tight enough to actually hurt, but enough to make me feel trapped. The figure was methodical, professional, like he'd done this hundreds of times before.

"You're doing so well, Britney. Your fear response is perfect. James is going to be thrilled with tonight's data."

Data. I was just data to them.

The drill sound stopped, replaced by the soft scrape of metal against concrete. The figure was moving around the room, setting up something I couldn't see.

"Now comes the interesting part," Dr. Sarah said. "We're going to see how long you can maintain your sanity when you truly believe you're going to die."

Something cold touched my neck—a blade, just resting against my skin. Not cutting, just. . . there. A promise of what could happen.

"This is where most people break completely," Dr. Sarah murmured. "The moment they realize that all their control, all their power, means nothing. That they're completely at our mercy."

The blade moved, tracing a line down my throat without breaking the skin. I could feel tears streaming down my face, though I hadn't realized I was crying.

"Perfect," Dr. Sarah breathed. "Just perfect. You're experiencing genuine terror now. The kind that changes people permanently."

I wanted to use the safe word. Every cell in my body was screaming at me to end this. But something deeper, something stubborn and angry, refused to give James Wylder the satisfaction.

"You know what the beautiful thing is?" Dr. Sarah continued. "After tonight, you'll never feel truly safe again. Every dark room, every unexpected sound, every moment when you're alone—you'll remember this. You'll remember how helpless you felt."

The figure leaned closer, his mask inches from my face. I could see his eyes through the holes—cold, empty, enjoying my fear.

"That's the gift we give people," Dr. Sarah whispered. "The knowledge of how easily they can be broken. How thin the line is between civilization and chaos."

A new sound filled the room—something like a chainsaw starting up. I knew it had to be fake, just another sound effect designed to terrify. But my body didn't know that. My body believed I was about to die.

"Last chance," Dr. Sarah said. "Say the word and it all stops. Refuse, and we see how far your mind can bend before it snaps."

I thought about James Wylder watching all of this, studying my reactions, getting off on my terror. The idea filled me with rage hot enough to burn through the fear.

"Go to hell," I whispered.

Dr. Sarah laughed. "Magnificent. You really are something special, Britney. Most people would have broken by now. But you. . . you're fighting even when you know it's hopeless."

The chainsaw sound got louder, closer. I could feel the vibration in the air, could smell exhaust fumes that had to be pumped in just for effect. Every horror movie cliché was being used against me.

"This is what real powerlessness feels like," Dr. Sarah said. "This is what it means to be completely at someone else's mercy. Remember this feeling, Britney. Remember how easy it was for us to reduce you to a terrified animal."

The sound stopped. The hands released me. The blade disappeared from my throat.

Suddenly, lights flooded the room. The figure stepped back and raised his hands in a non-threatening gesture. Dr. Sarah's voice returned to its warm, professional tone.

"Experience complete. Well done, Britney. You lasted fifty-seven minutes, which is impressive for a first-timer."

Seven

A DOOR OPENED IN the wall where there hadn't been one before, and Jennifer appeared with a warm smile and a bottle of water.

"How are you feeling?" she asked as she led me out of the basement and back toward the lobby.

"Fine," I managed, though I was shaking.

"It's normal to feel disoriented after an experience like that. The important thing is that you faced your fears and came through it."

As we walked, I tried to process what had just happened. James Wylder hadn't just created a horror attraction—he'd built a sophisticated psychological torture device. The monitoring, the customization, the way they pushed people past their breaking point—it was abuse disguised as therapy.

"The other participants should be finishing up soon," Jennifer said as we reached the lobby. "Then you can reunite with your fiancé for the cocktail reception."

I nodded, not trusting myself to speak. I needed to see Stu, needed to get out of this place. But first,

I had to survive the cocktail reception and James Wylder's inevitable debriefing.

He was going to want to know how I'd reacted, what I'd learned about myself, how the experience had "transformed" me.

What he didn't know was that it had transformed me—just not in the way he intended. I now understood how dangerous James Wylder was, and how much he deserved what was coming to him.

Jennifer handed me my phone back along with a small card. "Your personalized experience report," she explained. "It includes your biometric data, stress response patterns, and recommended follow-up sessions."

I glanced at the card. It looked like a medical report, with charts and graphs showing my heart rate, cortisol levels, and something called "fear threshold progression." At the bottom was a QR code and the words "Book your next transformation today."

These people were fucking sick.

"There's also a brief survey we'd love you to fill out," Jennifer continued, handing me a tablet. "Your feedback helps us improve the experience for future guests."

I scrolled through the questions, each one more invasive than the last. How would you rate your level of terror? Did you feel a sense of catharsis upon completion? Would you recommend this experience to others dealing with control issues? Have you ever experienced real trauma that compares to tonight's simulation?

I handed the tablet back without filling it out. "I'll need some time to process before I can give meaningful feedback."

"Of course. We encourage all our guests to reflect on their experience." Jennifer's smile never wavered. "Can I get you anything while we wait for the others? Perhaps some champagne?"

"Please."

The champagne helped steady my nerves, but I couldn't stop thinking about what I'd just endured. The way they'd isolated me, monitored my every reaction, pushed me to my breaking point—it was calculated cruelty. And judging by the satisfied expressions on the staff members' faces, they knew it.

Other guests began trickling back into the lobby, each looking as shaken as I felt. The tech guy was pale and sweating. The real estate developer kept checking her phone like she needed to confirm the outside world still existed. An older man in an expensive suit sat alone in a corner, staring at nothing.

But there was no sign of Stu.

"Excuse me," I said to Jennifer, who was floating between guests with practiced ease. "My fiancé hasn't come out yet. Should I be concerned?"

"Oh, don't worry," she replied. "Some experiences run longer than others. He should be out any moment."

Ten more minutes passed. Then fifteen. I was starting to pace when James Wylder himself appeared in the lobby, his face flushed with excitement.

"Britney!" he called out, striding over with arms spread wide like we were old friends. "How was it? I've been watching your biometrics—fascinating stuff."

The fact that he'd been watching me, studying my fear like a lab rat, made my skin crawl. But I forced a smile.

"Intense," I said. "Definitely not what I expected."

"The best experiences never are. You showed remarkable resilience—most people use the safe word by the forty-minute mark." James's eyes gleamed. "But you pushed through. That tells me a lot about your character."

"Such as?"

"You're someone who doesn't like to give up control. Even when you're terrified, even when every instinct is screaming at you to quit, you endure." He moved closer, lowering his voice. "That's rare. Most people break."

The way he said "break" made me want to break his fucking neck. But I needed to play the part a little longer.

"It was definitely a learning experience," I said.

"I'd love to discuss your reactions in more detail during the reception. I have some theories about your psychological profile that I think you'd find interesting."

Before I could respond, a door opened and Stu emerged, flanked by a different staff member. He looked composed, but I caught the tension in his shoulders, the way his eyes searched the room until they found mine.

"Stu!" James boomed, turning his attention to my fiancé. "How did you find your experience?"

"Educational," Stu replied, his voice carefully neutral.

"I'm sure it was. Law enforcement officers often have the most interesting responses to our scenarios. All that training in crisis management, but when you strip away the protocols and procedures. . ." James smiled. "Well, we're all just human underneath."

I could see tension in Stu's posture, but he kept his expression blank. "It certainly puts things in perspective."

"Great! Well, now that everyone's back, let's move to the reception area. I'm eager to hear everyone's thoughts."

James led our group through another set of doors into what looked like an upscale cocktail lounge. Soft lighting, leather seating areas, a full bar staffed by more attractive young people in black uniforms. It would have been elegant if I didn't know what lay behind the walls.

"Please, make yourselves comfortable," James announced. "Drinks are on the house, and I'll be circulating to chat with each of you about your experience."

I grabbed Stu's arm and steered him toward a quiet corner. "You okay?"

"Yeah. You?"

"I've been better." I kept my voice low. "What did they put you through?"

"Later," he murmured, glancing around. "Too many ears here."

He was right. James's staff was everywhere, mingling with guests, refilling drinks, asking casual questions about the experience. It was all very friendly and professional, but I could feel them listening, cataloging our responses.

"Britney, Stu," James appeared beside us with three glasses of what looked like expensive whiskey. "I wanted to thank you both personally for being here tonight. Your reactions have provided some valuable data."

"Data?" I asked.

"For our research. We're constantly refining the experiences based on participant feedback and biometric analysis." James handed us the glasses. "Your responses tonight were particularly interesting because they deviate from the typical patterns we see."

"How so?" Stu asked.

"Well, most business executives show a predictable fear response pattern—initial confidence, growing anxiety as control is removed, then either breakdown or angry resistance. But you, Britney, showed something different. Your stress indicators spiked, yes, but you also showed signs of. . . analysis. Like you were studying the experience even while experiencing it."

I felt a chill. He was more perceptive than I'd given him credit for.

"I suppose that's the consultant in me," I said. "Always looking at how systems work."

"Perhaps. Or perhaps you've experienced real powerlessness before. Trauma has a way of teaching us coping mechanisms." James's smile didn't reach his eyes. "What do you think, Stu? As someone who deals with victims of violent crime, would you say your fiancée shows signs of past trauma?"

The question hung in the air like a trap. James was fishing, trying to get under our skin, learn our vulnerabilities. I could see Stu calculating his response.

"I think," Stu said carefully, "that successful people often have experiences that teach them resilience. That's probably what you're seeing in the data."

"Hmm. Possibly." James didn't look convinced. "What about you? Your response pattern was even more unusual. Most law enforcement officers try to maintain control even in our scenarios—it's ingrained training. But you seemed to. . . surrender to the experience. Very zen-like."

"I've learned that sometimes the best strategy is to observe and adapt rather than fight."

"Interesting. And what did you observe?"

I held my breath, wondering how Stu would an-swer. We were walking a tightrope, trying to seem engaged without revealing too much.

"That you've created something very sophisti-cated," Stu said. "The level of psychological manip-ulation is impressive."

James beamed. "Thank you. Most people don't appreciate the technical artistry involved. The av-erage haunted house just throws actors in masks at you and hopes for the best. What we've built here is precision fear engineering."

"How did you develop the techniques?" I asked.

"Years of research. I studied everything—clin-ical psychology, interrogation methods, sensory deprivation, even looked at cult indoctrination practices. The goal was to understand how to break down psychological barriers in a controlled envi-ronment."

He was admitting to psychological torture like it was a hobby. I wanted to grab the whiskey glass and smash it across his face.

"That must have been disturbing research," Stu observed.

"Not at all. It was fascinating. Human psycholo-gy is predictable once you understand the underlying patterns. Everyone has breaking points. Everyone has fears they can't control. The trick is finding them and applying the right pressure."

"And what's the point?" I asked. "Beyond entertainment, I mean."

"Therapy, of course. But also research. We're learning things about human fear responses that could revolutionize psychology, law enforcement, even national security." James's eyes lit up. "Imagine being able to break down a terrorist's psychological defenses in hours instead of months. Or helping trauma victims by giving them controlled exposure to their triggers."

"Controlled exposure to trauma isn't a new concept," Stu said.

"Not the exposure—the breaking. Most therapy tries to help people cope with their fears. We help them shatter and rebuild stronger." James took a sip of his whiskey. "Destruction and rebirth. It's powerful."

I was starting to understand James Wylder's true pathology. He wasn't just sadistic—he was messianic. He believed he was helping people by tearing them apart psychologically. In his mind, the trauma he inflicted was a gift.

"Have you considered the ethical implications?" I asked.

"Of course. That's why we have all the safety measures, the monitoring, the safe words. No one gets hurt physically."

"What about psychologically?"

"Temporary distress in service of long-term growth. It's like surgery—sometimes you have to cut to heal."

The conversation was interrupted by a commotion near the bar. The real estate developer was arguing with one of the staff members, her voice getting louder.

"I want to leave. Now. This whole thing is sick."

"Ma'am, if you could just calm down—"

"Don't tell me to calm down! You people are insane!"

James excused himself and walked over to handle the situation. I watched as he spoke quietly to the woman, his demeanor shifting to something hypnotic. Within minutes, she was nodding, accepting another drink, allowing herself to be led to a couch.

"That was disturbing," Stu murmured.

"Everything about this place is disturbing." I finished my whiskey. "How much longer do we need to stay?"

"Not much longer. But we should mingle a bit more, ask some questions. The more we learn about his operation, the better."

For the next hour, we circulated through the reception, talking to other guests and staff members. The picture that emerged was worse than I'd imagined. James wasn't just running a horror attraction—he was conducting psychological experiments on paying customers.

The staff members were trained in manipulation techniques. The experiences were designed to create maximum psychological distress. And James was collecting detailed data on everyone who went through the attraction, building profiles of their fears, weaknesses, and breaking points.

"What does he do with all this information?" I asked Jennifer when I caught her alone at the bar.

"Research," she said. "Mr. Wylder is writing a book about fear psychology. He's also consulting with some government agencies about interrogation techniques."

My blood ran cold. James wasn't just torturing people for kicks—he was developing methods for professional torture and selling them to the highest bidder.

By the time we finally left Nightmares Unleashed, I was vibrating with rage. James had walked us to the valet stand personally, making small talk about future visits and research collaborations.

"I really hope you'll consider participating in our extended program," he said as we waited for our car. "Three-day intensive experiences that really allow for psychological breakthrough. I think you'd both be perfect candidates."

"We'll definitely consider it," I lied.

"Wonderful. I'll have Jennifer send you the information." James shook our hands with that same lingering grip. "Thank you again for being part of something special tonight."

As we drove away, I finally allowed myself to breathe. But the relief was temporary. Now that I understood what James Wylder really was, what he was really doing, I knew I couldn't let him continue.

He wasn't just exploiting people's trauma—he was weaponizing it.

And that made him the most dangerous kind of monster.

Eight

Neither of us spoke for the first ten minutes of the drive home. I stared out the passenger window, watching the city's lights blur past, trying to process everything I'd experienced. My hands were still shaking, and I gripped them together in my lap to keep them still.

Stu drove with focused intensity, his knuckles white on the steering wheel. Whatever they'd put him through had affected him too, though he was doing his usual stoic cop thing and keeping it buried.

"Jesus fucking Christ," I finally said, breaking the silence.

"Yeah." Stu's voice was rough. "That about covers it."

I turned to look at him. "What did they do to you?"

He was quiet for a moment, navigating around a slow-moving truck. "Police interrogation scenario. They had me tied to a chair while some asshole in a mask screamed questions about a case. Real case details they must have pulled from public records. Made it personal."

"How personal?"

"They knew about my father."

My blood chilled. Stu rarely talked about his dad, who'd been killed in the line of duty when Stu was twelve. It was part of what drove him to become a cop, and also one of his deepest wounds.

"Those sick fucks," I said.

"They had crime scene photos. Real ones, from his case file. I don't know how they got them, but. . ." He trailed off.

"Stu."

"They recreated it. The whole thing. Had an actor playing the shooter, with the same weapon, same everything. Made me watch it happen over and over while they questioned me about cases I'd worked."

I reached over and put my hand on his arm. "I'm sorry."

"The worst part? For a few minutes, I actually started to believe I was there. That I could save him this time if I just answered their questions right." He shook his head. "Fucked up."

We drove in silence again for a while. I was trying to reconcile the man I'd just spent an hour chatting with over whiskey—charming, articulate James Wylder—with someone who would orchestrate that level of psychological cruelty.

"He's not just a sadist," I said eventually.

"No?"

"He genuinely believes he's helping people. That's what makes him so dangerous." I told Stu about the messianic complex I'd recognized, about James's conviction that he was providing a service.

"The worst kind of monster," Stu agreed. "The kind that sleeps well at night."

"What did you think of his setup? Professionally, I mean."

Stu considered this. "Sophisticated as hell. The monitoring, the psychological profiling, the way they customize each experience—it's not amateur hour. Someone with serious training designed those protocols."

"The staff too. They're not just actors."

"No. That Jennifer woman knew what she was doing. And the way James handled that woman who wanted to leave. . ." Stu shook his head. "He had her eating out of his hand within minutes."

"Professional manipulation."

"Textbook stuff. The kind of techniques we learn about in hostage negotiation training, except he's using them to keep people from escaping his torture chamber."

We turned onto our street, and I felt some tension leave my shoulders. Home. Safety. Normal life where people didn't recreate your worst traumas for entertainment.

"So what's the plan?" Stu asked as we pulled into our driveway.

"I kill him, duh."

"Well, yeah, I know that. I meant the details."

I was quiet as we got out of the car and walked to the front door. Stu unlocked it, and we stepped inside to find Minion waiting in the entryway, her tiny black form silhouetted against the hallway light.

"Hey, baby girl," I said, scooping her up. She started purring and headbutting my chin, like she could sense I needed comfort.

"She missed us," Stu observed, scratching behind her ears.

"She always misses her mama. You? Maybe," I joked.

We headed to the kitchen, where I poured myself a large glass of wine and Stu grabbed a beer from the fridge. Minion wound around our legs, demanding attention after being left alone all evening.

"Okay," I said, settling onto the couch with Minion in my lap. "Here's what I'm thinking. This isn't going to be a quick kill. James Wylder is too high-profile, too connected. We need to be smart about it."

Stu sat beside me, close enough that I could feel his warmth. "What do you have in mind?"

"First, I need to learn everything about him. His routines, his security, his vulnerabilities. The preview event was just the beginning—I need to see how the whole operation works."

"You're thinking of going back?"

"Maybe. Or finding another way in. He mentioned that extended program—three days of intensive experiences. Could be an opportunity."

"Brit." Stu's voice carried a warning. "After tonight, you want to put yourself through more of that?"

"If it gets me close to him, yes." I took a sip of wine, feeling it burn slightly. "Besides, now I know what to expect. I can prepare mentally."

"And if he gets suspicious? He already thinks you're too analytical, remember? If you go back, he might start asking questions."

I considered this. Stu was right—James had been perceptive about my responses. Going back might raise red flags.

"Then I find another way," I said. "Maybe through his business connections. He mentioned government contracts—there might be a way to approach it from that angle."

"Risky. Government means background checks, scrutiny."

"Everything about this is risky." I shifted Minion to a more comfortable position, and she settled in with a contented sigh. "But I can't let him continue. You saw what he's doing to people. What he did to you."

Stu nodded slowly. "I know. And I'm with you, whatever you decide. But we need to be careful. This isn't like your other kills—this guy has resources, connections, security. If we fuck this up. . ."

"We won't." I leaned against him, feeling his solid presence. "We'll take our time, plan it right. And when it's done, the world will be rid of someone who gets off on breaking people for profit."

We sat in comfortable silence for a while, both lost in our thoughts. Minion had fallen asleep in my lap, her tiny body vibrating with purrs. The normalcy of it—sitting on our couch, our cat between us, having a drink after a long evening—felt surreal after what we'd experienced.

"I keep thinking about that woman," I said eventually. "The real estate developer. The way she knew something was wrong, tried to leave, and James just. . . manipulated her back into compliance."

"How many others has he done that to?"

"Hundreds, probably. And the data he's collecting on everyone. . ." I shuddered. "He's building profiles on people's deepest fears and vulnerabilities. What's he planning to do with all that information?"

"Nothing good." Stu finished his beer and set the empty bottle on the coffee table. "You ready for bed? It's been a long night."

I drained my wine glass and carefully transferred Minion to Stu's lap. "Yeah. I'm exhausted."

We headed upstairs, Minion trotting behind us. In the bedroom, I caught sight of myself in the mirror and was surprised by what I saw. I looked normal—a little tired, maybe, but not like someone who'd endured an hour of psychological torture.

"You okay?" Stu asked, noticing my expression.

"Just thinking about how well we hid it tonight. James had no idea who he was really dealing with."

"Good thing. If he knew what you were capable of. . ."

"He'd be running." I smiled grimly. "But he doesn't know. And by the time he figures it out, it'll be too late."

We got ready for bed in comfortable silence. Stu disappeared into the bathroom while I changed into pajamas—an old t-shirt and shorts that felt like armor after the evening's vulnerability.

When he came out, I took my turn, brushing my teeth and washing my face, trying to scrub away any lingering sense of James Wylder's presence. In the mirror, I practiced the expression I'd need tomorrow—businesswoman, temp agency owner, productive member of society. Not someone planning a murder.

When I emerged from the bathroom, Stu was in bed, propped up against the pillows with Minion curled on his chest. The sight made my heart clench with affection. This—this quiet domestic scene—was what I was protecting. What James Wylder threatened with his sick enterprise.

"Room for one more?" I asked.

"Always."

I slipped into bed beside them, and Minion repositioned herself between us, claiming the warm spot where our bodies met. Stu reached over and turned off the bedside lamp, plunging the room into darkness.

"Brit?"

"Yeah?"

"Tonight. . . what you went through down there. If you need to talk about it, or if it brings up anything about Dario. . ."

I was quiet for a moment, thinking about his offer. The basement experience had been terrifying, but not in the way Ben would worry about. It hadn't triggered memories of Dario so much as it had shown me exactly what kind of monster James Wylder was.

"I'm okay," I said finally. "Angry, but okay. What about you? The thing with your father. . ."

"I'll deal with it. I've had practice."

We lay in the dark, listening to Minion's purrs and the distant sound of traffic. I could feel Stu's breathing slow as he started to drift off, but my mind was still racing.

James Wylder thought he understood fear, thought he could control and manipulate it for his own purposes. He'd studied psychology and interrogation techniques, built a sophisticated operation designed to break people down and rebuild them according to his vision.

But he'd never met anyone like me. Someone who'd learned to channel fear into rage, rage into action. Someone who'd killed before and would kill again to protect the innocent.

"Stu?" I whispered.

"What?"

"When I kill him, I want him to know why. I want him to understand that his 'therapeutic terror' was nothing compared to real fear."

"You always make sure they know. I doubt this would be any different."

I smiled in the darkness, feeling Minion's warm weight against my side and Stu's protective presence beside me. Tomorrow I'd start planning James Wylder's death in earnest. I'd research his habits, his security, his vulnerabilities. I'd figure out how to get close enough to show him what real powerlessness felt like.

But tonight, I was home. Safe. Surrounded by the people—and cat—I loved most.

And that was enough.

Nine

I WOKE UP MONDAY morning with a plan.

Stu had already left for his early shift, and Minion was curled in the warm spot where he'd been sleeping. I lay there for a few minutes, letting my mind run through the details I'd worked out during the night.

James Wylder thought he was so clever with his psychological profiles and fear engineering. But he'd made one mistake—he'd let me inside his operation. Now I knew how it worked, who was involved, and most importantly, where he was vulnerable.

I fed Minion and made coffee, then grabbed my laptop from the kitchen table. First things first—I needed to do proper research on James without leaving digital footprints that could be traced back to me.

I drove to a coffee shop across town and used their Wi-Fi on a burner laptop I had just gotten for exactly these situations. James Wylder had a large online presence for someone running what amounted to a torture facility.

His LinkedIn showed connections to several government contractors, a handful of psychology professors, and what looked like private military companies. The guy wasn't just some amateur sadist—he had serious backing.

Smart move, James. No one would ever suspect.

His personal social media was more interesting. Lots of posts about "breakthrough therapeutic techniques" and "revolutionary approaches to trauma treatment." Photos from psychology conferences, articles he'd written for trade journals, and glimpses into his personal life.

He lived alone in a house in Hyde Park, drove a black BMW, and seemed to spend most of his free time either at the gym or at upscale restaurants downtown. No girlfriend that I could see, which made sense. Hard to maintain a relationship when your idea of helping people involved psychological torture.

But it was his speaking schedule that caught my attention. James was giving a presentation next week at the University of South Florida about "Innovative Approaches to Exposure Therapy." The event was open to psychology students and professionals.

Perfect.

I spent the next two hours mapping out everything I could find about his work routines, his security, his associates. Jennifer seemed to be his right hand, handling the business side while James focused on the "research." There were at least six other employees I could identify, all with backgrounds in psychology or theater.

By the time I headed to the office, I had the beginning of a plan.

"Morning, Britney," Barb chimed as I walked in. "You've got three messages and Julie wants to talk to you about the Morrison account."

"Thanks. I'll call her now."

I settled into my office and tried to focus on legitimate work. The Morrison account was a big law firm that wanted to expand their temp staff for a major case they were taking on. Normally, this kind of contract would have my attention.

Today, I kept thinking about James Wylder's presentation at USF.

I called Julie and we pulled up the Morrison contract in our shared database. "The Morrison people want to add two more paralegals and a receptionist to their original request," she said. "I've got candidates lined up, but they want to interview everyone this week."

"That's fast."

"They're starting trial prep next month. Big pharmaceutical liability case, apparently."

We spent twenty minutes going over the details in the system, and I forced myself to pay attention. This was my life, my business. I couldn't let my obsession with James interfere with the work that actually mattered.

But as soon as I hung up, I was back to planning.

The USF presentation was in a lecture hall that seated about two hundred people. I could register as a continuing education student—I had a bachelor's degree in business, which would be enough to justify my interest in psychology courses.

More importantly, the event was being held in the evening, and there was a reception afterward for attendees to "network with professionals in the field."

Another opportunity to get close to James without raising suspicion.

My phone buzzed with a text from an unknown number: *Hope you're still thinking about our extended program. I have some ideas for your next experience. —James*

I stared at the message, feeling that familiar mix of rage and calculation. He was fishing, trying to keep me engaged with his operation. The fact that he was texting me personally instead of having Jennifer do it meant I'd made an impression.

Good. That would make this easier.

I screenshot the message and sent it to Stu, then typed back: *Very interested. What did you have in mind?*

His response came back within minutes: *Something more personalized. We could design an experience specifically around your relationship dynamics. Couples therapy through controlled trauma. Very cutting edge.*

I had to grip my phone to keep from throwing it across the room. This fucking prick wanted to torture Stu and me together, probably get off on watching our relationship dynamics under stress.

Sounds intriguing. Can we discuss it in person sometime?

I'm giving a presentation at USF next week. Perhaps we could meet afterward? I'd love to hear your thoughts on exposure therapy methodologies.

Perfect. He was making this almost too easy.

I'd love to attend. What's the topic?

Innovative Approaches to Exposure Therapy. Wednesday at 7 PM, Cooper Hall. I'll put you on the guest list.

Looking forward to it.

I set my phone down and leaned back in my chair. Phase one was complete. I had a legitimate reason to be at his presentation, and an excuse to approach him afterward.

Now I needed to figure out how to use that access to get him alone.

The rest of the day crawled by. I handled client calls, reviewed contracts, and tried to act like someone whose biggest concern was temporary staffing solutions. But my mind kept drifting to Wednesday night.

James thought he understood fear, thought he could control and manipulate it for his own purposes. He'd built an entire business around breaking people down and convincing them it was thera-peutic.

But he'd never met someone like me. Someone who'd learned to turn fear into rage, and rage into action.

Stu got home around six, looking tired after what was a long day of calls.

"How was work?" I asked, kissing him as he set his keys on the counter.

"Same shit, different day. Three DV calls, two drug arrests, and one guy who thought his neighbor was stealing his newspaper." He opened the fridge and grabbed a beer. "How about you? You look like you've been plotting."

"Maybe." I told him about James's text messages and the USF presentation.

"You sure about this? Getting close to him again?"

"I need to see how he operates outside his controlled environment. The presentation will give me a chance to observe him with other people, see how he presents himself to the academic community."

"And after?"

"I'll figure out a way to get him alone. Maybe suggest we continue the conversation somewhere private."

Stu was quiet for a moment, drinking his beer and thinking. "What if he gets suspicious? You show up at his presentation right after experiencing his attraction—that might seem like more than coincidence."

"I'll play it as professional interest. Successful business owner looking to understand psychology for better employee management. It's not that far from the truth."

"And if he tries something?"

I smiled. "Then he'll learn the difference between controlled fear and the real thing."

We made dinner together—pasta with marinara sauce, nothing fancy but comforting after the stress of the past few days. Minion supervised from her perch on the counter, reaching out a paw to bat at the steam rising from the pot.

"You know what I keep thinking about?" I said as we sat down to eat.

"What?"

"I'm still stuck on that woman who tried to leave. The real estate developer. She knew something was wrong, trusted her instincts, and James just. . . erased all of that within minutes."

"Professional technique. Guy knows what he's doing."

"But that's just it—he does know what he's doing. This isn't some amateur operation. He's got serious training, serious backing, and he's using it to systematically break people down for profit."

"You think he's done this before? Before Nightmares Unleashed?"

"I think James Wylder has been perfecting these techniques for years. The attraction is just his latest laboratory."

We finished dinner and settled on the couch to watch Mindhunter. But I couldn't concentrate. My mind kept running through scenarios for Wednesday night, trying to anticipate every possible outcome.

James thought he was the predator in this situation. He thought he was the one with the power, the one in control.

He was about to learn how wrong he was.

Around ten, my phone buzzed with another message from James: *Been thinking about your psychological profile. You show remarkable resilience, but I suspect there are deeper vulnerabilities we haven't explored yet. The couples experience would be perfect for that.*

I showed Stu the message. "He's not going to give up."

"Good. Let him think he's reeling you in. The more confident he gets, the sloppier he'll be."

I typed back: *You certainly know how to intrigue someone. I'm very interested in hearing more about your methods.*

Wednesday can't come soon enough. I have a feeling you're going to love what I have planned.

I smiled as I set my phone aside. James Wylder thought he was the one setting a trap.

But he had no idea he was walking into mine.

Ten

Tuesday dragged by like a death sentence.

I tried to focus on work, but every client call felt like background noise. Barb noticed my restlessness and kept sending messages to check if I was okay. Even Minion seemed to pick up on my energy when I got home—she spent the evening following me around the house like a tiny black shadow.

"You're going to pace a hole in the floor," Stu said, watching me make my fourth lap around the living room.

"I can't sit still." I dropped onto the couch beside him. "Tomorrow night feels like a test, and I hate tests. None of my other kills have felt like this."

"You're overthinking it. It's just a presentation. You go, you listen, you talk to him afterward. Nothing dramatic."

Easy for you to say. You're not the one walking into the lion's den.

"What if he gets suspicious? What if he realizes I'm not who I'm pretending to be?"

Stu turned off the TV and faced me. "Brit, you've been lying to people your whole life. You're good at it. Tomorrow won't be different."

He was right, but that didn't stop the anxious energy crackling under my skin. I'd killed six people, and none of them had required this level of planning. This level of risk.

But none of them had been like James Wylder.

Wednesday morning, I woke up before my alarm. Stu was already gone—another early shift—and I had the house to myself. I made coffee and sat at the kitchen table, going over my plan one more time.

I'd registered for the presentation using my real name and business credentials. Britney Cage, owner of Passing Through Temp Agency, interested in understanding workplace psychology for better employee management. It was a solid cover story, close enough to the truth that I wouldn't trip over details.

The day at the office crawled by. I handled three client calls, reviewed two contracts, and had a brief meeting with Julie about expanding our services to include more specialized placements. All normal, mundane business that felt surreal when I knew what I'd be doing in a few hours.

"You seem distracted today," Barb said when she brought me the afternoon messages. "Everything okay?"

"Fine. Just thinking about a presentation I'm attending tonight."

"Work-related?"

"Psychology seminar. Thought it might help with employee relations."

Barb nodded approvingly. "That's smart. Understanding what makes people tick is half the battle in our business."

If only she knew how well I understood what made people tick.

I left the office at four and drove home to change. I'd dressed carefully—professional but not too formal. Black slacks, cream blouse, blazer that could hide the small knife I always carried and my distinctive arm tattoos. Just another business owner looking to expand her knowledge.

Just another predator stalking more dangerous prey.

The presentation started at seven, but I wanted to get there early, scope out the location, see how James interacted with people before his guard was up.

USF's campus was buzzing with evening students heading to night classes. Cooper Hall was easy to find—a modern building with sleek glass facades and the kind of imposing design that screamed "we take ourselves very seriously here, but we also have fun."

The lecture hall was already half full when I arrived at six-thirty. I grabbed a seat in the middle section, close enough to see James clearly but not so close that I'd stand out. The audience was a mix of graduate students, working professionals, and curious faculty members.

Perfect cover. Just another face in the crowd.

James arrived at six-forty-five, and My heart rate spiked. He looked different here than he had at Nightmares Unleashed—more academic, less predatory. He wore a navy suit with a crisp white shirt, his salt-and-pepper hair perfectly styled. He carried himself with the confidence of someone who knew he belonged on that stage.

Such a good actor. Wonder how many people he's fooled with that respectable professor routine.

He spent a few minutes setting up his presentation, chatting with department faculty. I watched him laugh at something one of them said, saw how easily he slipped into the role of respected researcher. No one here would ever suspect what he really was.

The presentation started promptly at seven. James's topic was "Innovative Approaches to Exposure Therapy: Bridging the Gap Between Traditional Methods and Immersive Experience."

"Immersive experience." That's one way to describe it.

For the next hour, I watched James Wylder give one of the most disturbing presentations I'd ever seen, disguised as legitimate academic research.

He talked about the limitations of traditional exposure therapy, how patients often failed to engage fully with their fears in clinical settings. He presented data showing higher success rates with "immersive, controlled fear experiences" compared to standard talk therapy approaches.

Using his victims' terror as research data. Sick bastard.

The worst part was how compelling he was. He spoke with passion about helping people overcome trauma, about revolutionary treatment methods that could change the field of psychology. Several audience members took notes. A few asked thoughtful questions about implementation and ethics oversight.

If I didn't know what I did, I might have been impressed, too.

"The key," James said, advancing to a slide showing brain scans, "is creating fear responses that are intense enough to trigger genuine psychological processing, but controlled enough to ensure patient safety. We've found that traditional clinical settings simply can't replicate the necessary stress conditions."

A woman in the front row raised her hand. "Dr. Wylder, how do you address concerns about re-traumatization? Some of these methods seem quite aggressive."

James smiled—that same charming smile I'd seen him use on the real estate developer. "That's an excellent question. The difference between re-traumatization and therapeutic breakthrough is all about control. In our facility, every variable is monitored and adjusted in real-time. We can push patients to their psychological edge without pushing them over it."

Bullshit. You push people over the edge and call it therapy.

"We also use extensive pre-screening and post-treatment follow-up to ensure positive outcomes," he continued. "Our success rates speak for themselves."

More lies. He had no idea what happened to people after they left his torture chamber. He just took their money and moved on to the next victim.

The presentation wrapped up at eight, followed by polite applause. James invited the audience to stay for the reception in the lobby, where he'd be available for questions and further discussion.

Showtime.

I waited for the initial crowd around James to thin out before approaching. He was talking to a young graduate student about internship opportunities when I stepped up.

"James."

His face lit up. "Britney! You made it. I wasn't sure you'd be able to get away from the office on such short notice."

"Fascinating. Your approach to controlled fear exposure is unlike anything I've heard before. I'd love to hear more about your facility. The technical aspects of how you monitor and adjust the experiences in real-time."

"I'd be happy to discuss it. Perhaps we could continue this conversation somewhere more private? The coffee shop across campus stays open late."

Perfect. Getting him alone was easier than I'd expected.

"That sounds great."

We walked across campus in the cool evening air, James talking enthusiastically about his research and methods. He was in full professorial mode, clearly enjoying having an interested audience for his work.

Keep talking, asshole. The more you tell me, the better I'll understand your operation.

The coffee shop was nearly empty, just a few students with laptops and textbooks scattered around. We found a quiet table in the back corner, and James got us coffee while I settled in to listen to him incriminate himself.

"So," he said, sitting down across from me, "tell me more about your interest in workplace psychology. Your response to our experience was quite unique."

"I manage a lot of different personality types in my business. Understanding what motivates people, what scares them, what makes them perform better—it's all relevant."

"And you felt our methods gave you insight into those dynamics?"

Oh, they gave me insight all right. Insight into what a monster you are.

"Definitely. The level of psychological pressure you can create in a controlled environment is remarkable. I imagine it reveals things about people that they might not even know about themselves."

James leaned forward, his eyes lighting up. "Exactly! That's what separates our approach from traditional therapy. We don't just talk about fears—we make people live them. The psychological revelations that emerge from genuine terror are unlike anything you can achieve in a clinical setting."

"Have you considered expanding beyond individual treatments? The couples therapy concept you mentioned seems particularly innovative."

"That's still in development, but yes—the relationship dynamics that emerge under stress are extraordinary. We can identify communication patterns, power structures, hidden resentments that might take years to surface in traditional therapy."

Or you can torture two people at once and get off on watching their relationship implode.

"How do you ensure consent in those situations? It seems like it could be easy for one partner to pressure the other into participating."

James waved dismissively. "We have extensive screening processes. Both partners have to demonstrate genuine commitment to the therapeutic process. And our monitoring systems would catch any signs of coercion."

Like you coerced the real estate developer to stay?

We talked for another hour, James becoming more animated as he described his methods. He showed me photos of his facility on his phone, pointed out technical features of the monitoring systems, even mentioned some of the government contracts he was pursuing.

He's so proud of his torture chamber. Practically preening.

By the time we parted ways at ten-thirty, I had more information than I'd dared hope for. James had given me his personal cell number, invited me to tour his facility during operational hours, and suggested we set up a time to discuss the couples experience in detail.

He thought he was grooming his next victim, not planning his own death.

Driving home, I felt that familiar calm settle over me. The same feeling I'd had before killing Dario, before disposing of Katie. The certainty that came with knowing someone needed to die, and knowing I was the one who would make it happen.

James Wylder had shown me exactly who he was tonight. A predator who used academic credentials and therapeutic language to justify torture. A man who collected people's deepest fears and vulnerabilities like trophies.

Tomorrow I'd start planning the specifics. But tonight, for the first time in days, I felt at peace.

Sleep well, James. You don't have many nights left.

Eleven

Thursday morning arrived with the kind of crisp clarity that felt like a good omen. I woke up refreshed for the first time in days, the anxious energy replaced by calm focus.

Stu was already gone, but he'd left coffee in the pot and a note on the counter: *You've got this. Love you.*

I smiled despite myself. Even when he didn't know the specifics, he always seemed to understand what I needed to hear.

I took my coffee and headed to the office. Barb was already there, sorting through the morning messages with her usual efficiency.

"Morning," I said, settling into my chair. "Anything urgent?"

"Just the usual. A few follow-up calls from yesterday's placements and one new client inquiry."

"Perfect. Hold my calls for the first hour unless it's an emergency. I need to do some research."

Barb nodded and closed my door behind her. I opened my laptop and got to work. Time to do some real research on Dr. James Wylder.

The university website gave me his office hours, teaching schedule, and research interests. His LinkedIn showed speaking engagements, academic conferences, and a carefully curated professional image. But it was his personal social media that proved most useful.

James wasn't particularly active online, but what he did post painted a picture of his routines. Photos from his morning runs through Bayshore Boulevard - the same route I took most mornings, though I'd never seen him. Check-ins at the same coffee shop near campus. Pictures from faculty mixers and academic events.

Creatures of habit. Makes my job easier.

I spent the next hour mapping out his schedule based on what I could piece together. He taught two classes on Tuesdays and Thursdays, held office hours on Wednesdays and Fridays, and seemed to favor the same restaurants for lunch meetings.

But Nightmares Unleashed was where the real opportunity lay. James had invited me to tour the facility, and I'd be an idiot not to take him up on it. I needed to see the place in operation, understand the layout, figure out where he was most vulnerable.

I pulled out my phone and scrolled to his contact. He'd texted me yesterday afternoon, following up on our coffee conversation.

Thanks again for such an engaging discussion last night. I'd love to show you our facility in action.

Are you free Saturday the 29th? We have a couples session scheduled that might interest you.

Perfect. A couples session would give me the perfect cover to observe how he operated when he thought he was in complete control.

I typed back: *The 29th works perfectly. Looking forward to seeing your methods in practice.*

His response came within minutes: *Excellent. The session starts at 8 PM. I'll send you the address and security codes. Fair warning - what you'll see might be intense, but I think you'll find it fascinating from a psychological perspective.*

I'm sure I will.

If only he knew just how fascinating I'd find it.

I spent the rest of the morning working on legitimate business, handling client calls and reviewing contracts. But my mind kept drifting to Saturday the 29th. To James in his element, thinking he was showing off his revolutionary therapy to a potential ally.

Around noon, my phone rang. Julie.

"Hey, stranger. How's the psychology seminar treating you?"

I'd forgotten I'd told her about attending the presentation. "Educational. Really opened my eyes to some new approaches."

"That's great! Listen, I wanted to run something by you. That new client we landed - they're asking about employee psychological profiling for better team dynamics. I thought maybe you could use some of what you learned?"

The irony wasn't lost on me. "Send me the details. I might have some insights."

We chatted for a few more minutes about business before she hung up. Normal life continuing while I planned my next kill. The duality never stopped amusing me.

I left the office early again, claiming I had another seminar to attend. Barb was starting to give me curious looks, but she didn't ask questions. One of the many reasons I kept her around.

At home, I changed into workout clothes and decided to take a drive past Nightmares Unleashed. In daylight, it looked like any other commercial building - nondescript, professional, giving no hint of what happened inside after dark.

Could be the perfect place to kill him. His own torture chamber turned against him.

I parked across the street and watched for a while. A few cars came and went, probably staff preparing for evening sessions. James's BMW wasn't there, which meant he was likely still on campus.

Saturday the 29th, shitbag. Then I'll see exactly what kind of monster you really are.

I drove home feeling more centered than I had in days. The planning phase was always my favorite part - the chess game of positioning pieces before the final move.

Stu got home around six, exhausted from another long shift. I had dinner ready, something simple but filling. He looked surprised.

"You're in a good mood," he observed, settling into his chair.

"Had a productive day. Made some progress on a project I've been working on."

"The psychology stuff?"

"Something like that."

He didn't push for details. Another reason I loved him - he understood that sometimes I needed to work through things in my own way.

After dinner, we settled on the couch to watch TV. I curled up against his side, feeling the steady rhythm of his breathing. This was what normal felt like. What peace felt like.

But underneath that calm, excitement hummed through my veins. Saturday the 29th was still over a week away. Over a week until I'd be inside James Wylder's operation, seeing him in action.

Over a week until I'd start planning how to destroy him.

"Penny for your thoughts," Stu murmured against my hair.

"Just thinking about the weekend," I said truthfully.

"Want to do something fun? We could take the boat out Sunday if the weather's nice."

I smiled. "That sounds perfect."

It really did. A nice, peaceful Sunday on the water after I finished my reconnaissance mission. The contrast felt fitting somehow - death and life, violence and peace, all part of the same twisted tapestry that made up my world.

Two weeks, James. Then we'll see who's really in control.

Twelve

I KNEW THE DAYS between now and the 29th would move slow as molasses. I threw myself into work, handling client after client, but my mind kept wandering to James and what I'd see at Nightmares Unleashed.

Friday morning brought rain, which matched my restless mood. I sat in my office watching it streak down the windows, thinking about how different this hunt would be from the others.

"You're doing it again," Barb said from my doorway.

"Doing what?"

"Staring off into space. You've been distracted all week." She stepped into my office and closed the door behind her. "Everything okay?"

I forced a smile. "Just thinking about a new project. Nothing to worry about."

Barb didn't look convinced, but she dropped it. One of the reasons I kept her around - she knew when not to push.

Around lunch, Julie called.

"Girls' night tomorrow? Sarah's been asking when we're getting together again, and I could use the distraction. Brian's sleeping over at a friend's house."

Perfect. A normal Friday night out would help me blend back into regular life before Saturday's reconnaissance mission.

"The Pub at seven-thirty?"

"Actually, I was thinking we could try that new place in Hyde Park. Mezze 119. Change of scenery?"

"Sounds good."

The rest of Friday passed without incident. I handled three client calls, reviewed two contracts, and even had time to catch up on invoicing. Normal business owner stuff that felt surreal when I knew what I'd be doing tomorrow night.

Girls' night at Mezze 119 was exactly what I needed - a few hours of wine and conversation that had nothing to do with murder or psychology or James Wylder. Julie looked relaxed for the first time in weeks, Sarah was her usual chatty self, and even Barb seemed to be settling into our group dynamic.

"So what's this psychology seminar you keep mentioning?" Sarah asked over her second glass of wine.

"Just some workplace management stuff," I said, twirling pasta around my fork. "Understanding what makes people tick."

"Sounds boring," Julie laughed.

You have no idea.

We spent two hours catching up, gossiping about clients, and planning our next get-together. Normal friend stuff that felt both comforting and strange when I knew what I'd be doing the next night.

Saturday morning, I woke up with nervous energy crackling under my skin. Stu had already left for work, but he'd left another note: *Good luck with your seminar tonight. Love you.*

Poor guy had no clue what I was really doing.

I spent the rest of the morning doing normal Saturday things - grocery shopping, cleaning the house, taking Minion to the vet for her routine check-up. All the mundane activities that made up the life of Britney Cage, respectable business owner.

But underneath it all, anticipation hummed through my veins.

Around four, I started getting ready. James had sent me the address and security codes yesterday, along with detailed instructions about where to park and which entrance to use. The couples session was scheduled for eight, but he wanted me there by seven-thirty.

I dressed carefully - dark jeans, black long-sleeved shirt, comfortable boots. Nothing that would stand out. I slipped my knife into its usual place and checked that my phone was fully charged.

Time to see what you're really about, James.

The drive to Nightmares Unleashed took twenty minutes through Saturday evening traffic. The building looked different at night - more imposing, with strategically placed lighting that created shadows around the perimeter.

I parked where James had instructed and walked to the side entrance. The security code worked perfectly, and I slipped inside.

The interior was sleek and modern, all brushed steel and dark colors. Nothing like the cheesy haunted house I'd been expecting. This looked more like a medical facility, which made it more unsettling.

"Britney!" James appeared from around a corner, wearing dark slacks and a black polo shirt. His professional demeanor was still there, but there was something else in his eyes now. Excitement.

"Thanks for coming. I think you're going to find this educational."

"I'm sure I will."

He led me down a hallway lined with observation windows, each one tinted dark. The rooms beyond were mostly empty now, but I could make out equipment - cameras, monitors, speakers.

"These are our individual therapy suites," James explained. "Each one is customized based on the client's specific psychological profile. Tonight we're using the couples therapy room."

We stopped in front of a door marked "Observation Suite A." James entered a code and ushered me inside.

The room was set up like a control center, with multiple monitors showing different camera angles. There were audio controls, environmental controls, even what looked like lighting controls.

"Impressive setup," I said, and meant it. This wasn't some amateur operation.

"We spared no expense," James said proudly. "Complete environmental control is essential for psychological breakthrough."

Breakthrough. Sure.

"And tonight's couple?"

"Married fifteen years. Communication issues since their youngest left for college. Traditional therapy wasn't helping."

I watched James's face as he talked about them. There was something there - not concern or empathy, but anticipation. Like he was looking forward to a show.

For the next hour, I observed the intake process, watched James interact with his staff, noted the security measures and camera placements. I asked questions about the process, showed appropriate interest in his methods.

But mostly, I watched James. How he moved through the space, where he felt most comfortable, what made him animated and what made him cautious.

By the time the session started, I had a dozen new pieces of information about his operation. Not enough to plan a kill, but enough to know this place held possibilities.

The actual couples session was disturbing in ways I hadn't expected. Not because it was overtly violent, but because of how calculated it was. How James manipulated the environment to push the couple toward breaking points.

"Fascinating," I murmured at one point, and James beamed like I'd given him the highest compliment.

You sick fuck.

When it was over, James walked me to my car.

"So what did you think? Could you see applications for your business?"

"Absolutely. The psychological insights were remarkable." I unlocked my car. "I'd love to see more of your individual sessions sometime."

"Of course. I'll send you our schedule. We have several interesting cases coming up."

I drove home feeling like I'd stepped into a different world. James's operation was more sophisticated than I'd expected, which meant killing him would require more planning than usual.

But it also meant he had more to lose. More ways to make him suffer before the end.

This is going to be fun.

Thirteen

Sunday morning, I woke up before Stu again. Last night felt like a dream - or maybe a nightmare, depending on how you looked at it. I'd seen enough of James's operation to know he was worse than I'd imagined, but not enough to plan his death yet.

I made coffee and sat on the back patio with Minion, watching her chase lizards in the morning sun. Normal Sunday stuff, except my mind kept replaying scenes from Nightmares Unleashed.

The way James had watched that couple suffer. The excitement in his eyes when the woman started crying. The clinical detachment as he adjusted environmental controls to push them harder.

Twisted piece of shit.

My phone buzzed with a text from James.

Thanks again for last night. Hope you found it as educational as I did fascinating. I'll send you our schedule for the week - we have some particularly interesting individual cases coming up.

I typed back: *Your methods are unlike anything I've encountered. Should provide valuable insights.*

That much was true.

Stu came downstairs around nine, still groggy from his late shift. He found me on the patio with my coffee.

"Morning," he mumbled, kissing the top of my head. "How was your seminar?"

"Eye-opening." I set my mug down. "Want to take the boat out today? Weather's perfect."

His face lit up. "Hell yes. Give me thirty minutes to wake up properly."

We spent the morning on the water, just the two of us and the endless expanse of Tampa Bay. Stu handled the boat while I lounged in the sun, letting the normal rhythm of waves and wind wash away the lingering unease from last night.

"You seem relaxed," Stu observed as we anchored near a sandbar.

"I am. This is exactly what I needed."

It was true. Being out here, away from everything, reminded me why I loved this life. The balance between darkness and light, violence and peace. Soon I'd be planning James's death, but today I could just be Britney Cage, woman in love, enjoying a Sunday on the water.

We stayed out until late afternoon, anchoring at different spots around the bay. Stu caught two decent-sized snapper, and I managed to hook a small grouper that we threw back. Normal couple stuff that felt good after the twisted shit I'd witnessed at Nightmares Unleashed.

"You're quiet today," Stu said as we headed back to the marina.

"Just relaxed. Yesterday was intense."

"The seminar?"

"Yeah. Heavy stuff about trauma and psychological triggers." Not entirely a lie. "Made me appreciate this even more."

I gestured at the water, the sky, the simple pleasure of being with him.

Back home, we grilled the snapper on the back patio while Minion prowled around our feet, hoping for scraps. Stu opened a bottle of wine, and we settled into the outdoor furniture as the sun started to set.

"So what exactly did you learn at this seminar?" he asked, cutting into his fish.

I'd been expecting this question. "New approaches to understanding what drives people. How stress reveals true personality traits." I sipped my wine. "Might help with difficult clients."

"Makes sense. You deal with all types at the agency."

We ate in comfortable silence for a while, the evening air cooling around us. I watched Stu enjoy his fish, completely relaxed and content, and felt that familiar pang of love mixed with guilt. He had no idea what I was really planning.

"Want to watch that show tonight?" he asked. "The one we started last week?"

"Perfect."

We cleaned up dinner together, then settled on the couch with Minion between us. Stu found our show while I pretended to pay attention, but my mind kept drifting to James. To that couple from last night, and what they might be dealing with today after his "breakthrough therapy."

Probably traumatized worse than when they started.

"You okay?" Stu asked during a commercial break. "You still seem distracted."

"Just tired. You know what a long day on the water does to me."

He pulled me closer against his side. "Early night?"

"In a few minutes."

But I wasn't tired. My mind was too active, processing everything I'd seen, planning my next moves. James had texted about scheduling more observations, and I needed to be strategic about which sessions would give me the most useful intelligence.

We watched another episode before heading upstairs. Stu was asleep within minutes of his head hitting the pillow, but I lay awake staring at the ceiling.

Tomorrow I'd start the real work. The careful, methodical process of learning James's routines, his vulnerabilities, his weaknesses. Saturday night had been just the beginning.

Sweet dreams, you degenerate fuck. Enjoy them while you can.

Monday brought me back to reality. James had sent his schedule as promised, and I spent the morning studying it between client calls. Three individual sessions this week, plus another couples session on Friday.

Friday's too soon. Need to see more first.

Around lunch, Barb knocked on my door.

"Julie's on line two. Says it's about the Henderson contract."

I picked up. "What's the Henderson situation?"

"They want to extend Sarah's placement through the end of the month. Something about a big project coming up." Julie paused. "But Sarah mentioned she might have some availability issues."

Sarah worked part-time for us while finishing her master's degree. Smart girl, but her schedule could be tricky.

"What kind of availability issues?"

"Thesis defense is coming up. She needs more flexibility for prep time."

We spent ten minutes working out a modified schedule that would keep Henderson happy and give Sarah the time she needed. Normal business stuff that felt strange when part of my brain was still analyzing James's security cameras and exit routes.

After hanging up, I pulled up James's schedule again. Tuesday evening had an individual session - a young man dealing with "authority figure trauma." The clinical description made my stomach turn.

He's going to torture some kid who probably just needs actual therapy.

I texted James: *Would Tuesday evening's session be appropriate for observation? I'm particularly interested in individual treatment approaches.*

His response came within minutes: *Perfect timing. This case should provide excellent insights into breakthrough techniques. 7 PM start time.*

Excellent. I'm particularly interested in how you handle resistance during individual sessions.

The rest of Monday crawled by. I handled three client calls, reviewed two contracts, and had a brief meeting with Julie about expanding our services. All normal business that felt surreal when I knew what I'd be doing tomorrow night.

Tuesday morning brought rain again, matching my mood. I sat in my office going over James's facility layout in my mind, noting security measures and potential vulnerabilities. Not enough information yet to plan anything concrete, but pieces were starting to form.

Barb brought me the morning messages around ten.

"Ben Peterson called again. Still wants to discuss that contract amendment."

"Right. I'll call him back this afternoon."

"Also, your one o'clock canceled. Car trouble."

Perfect. That gave me time to drive by James's house in broad daylight, see his neighborhood, maybe spot his daily routines.

I left the office at twelve-thirty, claiming I needed to scout a new client location. Not entirely a lie - James was definitely a new client, just not the kind Barb would expect.

His house was in Westchase, a newer subdivision with wide streets and minimal privacy between homes. Not ideal for what I had planned, but good to know. I drove past twice, noting his BMW in the driveway, security system signs in the yard, and the general flow of neighborhood traffic.

Too exposed for anything dramatic. But good intel.

Back at the office, I spent the afternoon on legitimate business, but my mind kept drifting to tonight. To James in his element again, manipulating some poor kid's trauma for his own twisted research.

By five o'clock, anticipation was humming through my veins again. Time to see just how deep James's rabbit hole went.

Round two, asshole. Let's see what else you've got.

Fourteen

JAMES WAS WAITING FOR me in the observation room when I arrived Tuesday night, looking pleased to see me.

"Britney! Right on time. Tonight's going to be particularly illuminating."

"I'm sure it will be."

He gestured to the monitors showing the individual therapy suite. It was smaller than the couples room, more intimate. More claustrophobic.

"Our subject is twenty-three, college dropout, history of abuse from a stepfather. Classic authority figure trauma presenting as anxiety and panic attacks."

Subject. Not patient. Not client. Subject.

"And your approach?"

"Controlled exposure to authority scenarios. We'll gradually increase the pressure until we achieve breakthrough."

I watched the monitors as a young man was led into the room. He looked scared already, fidgeting with his hands, glancing around nervously at the cameras.

Poor kid has no idea what he's in for.

"The beauty of individual sessions," James continued, "is the level of control we can maintain. No outside variables, no partner dynamics to complicate the process."

For the next two hours, I watched James systematically break down a traumatized young man in the name of therapy. What I witnessed made Saturday night's couples session look like a picnic.

The kid - Marcus, according to his intake form - had come seeking help for panic attacks that were interfering with his life. Instead, James put him through a series of scenarios designed to trigger his worst memories. Role-playing exercises with staff members posing as authority figures. Environmental controls that created the sensation of being trapped.

At one point, Marcus tried to leave. Just stood up and walked toward the door. James calmly activated some kind of magnetic lock, trapping him inside while explaining over the intercom that "resistance was part of the breakthrough process."

"Fascinating," I murmured, and James beamed like I'd given him the highest compliment.

You sadistic motherfucker.

When it was over, Marcus was led out looking worse than when he'd arrived. Shaking, pale, eyes darting around like he expected another attack at any moment.

"Remarkable progress," James said, making notes on his tablet. "You can see how the controlled stress environment reveals underlying psychological patterns."

"Absolutely. The psychological insights were remarkable."

You just destroyed that kid for your own amusement.

I drove home from Nightmares Unleashed with my hands gripping the steering wheel tighter than necessary. What I'd witnessed tonight made Saturday's couples session look like child's play.

The young man - barely out of college, traumatized by years of abuse - had walked into that room looking for help. He'd walked out broken in new ways James probably called "therapeutic breakthrough."

Fucking degenerate piece of...

By the time I pulled into my driveway, it was almost ten-thirty. The house was dark except for the blue glow of the TV through the living room window. Stu would be on the couch, probably asleep with some documentary still playing.

I found him exactly where I'd expected, remote dangling from his hand, mouth slightly open. Minion was curled up on his chest, purring. For a moment I just stood there watching them - this simple, peaceful scene that felt a million miles away from what I'd just witnessed.

"Hey," Stu mumbled, blinking awake as I sat down beside him. "How was your seminar?"

"Disturbing." Not a lie. "Some people shouldn't be allowed to practice therapy."

He sat up straighter, dislodging Minion, who shot me an annoyed look. "Bad presenter?"

"You could say that." I kicked off my boots and tucked my feet under me. "What are you watching?"

"Something about deep sea creatures. Fell asleep twenty minutes in."

We sat in comfortable silence for a while, Stu's arm around my shoulders, the TV showing footage of bizarre fish in crushing darkness. The irony wasn't lost on me - down in those depths, predators lurked in the shadows, hunting prey that never saw them coming.

Just like James. Just like me.

"You okay?" Stu asked. "You seem tense."

"Just processing what I learned tonight. Some heavy psychological stuff."

He squeezed my shoulder. "Want to talk about it?"

"Not really. Just glad to be home."

We headed upstairs around eleven. Stu was asleep within minutes, but I lay awake staring at the ceiling, replaying every detail from tonight. James's excitement as he manipulated the environment. The clinical notes he'd taken while watching the kid suffer. The way he'd explained his "methodology" like he was discussing the weather.

I needed more information before I could plan his death properly. More sessions, more time to study his routines, more chances to find his weaknesses.

But patience had never been my strong suit.

Wednesday morning brought gray skies and the kind of humidity that made your clothes stick to your skin. I got to the office early, hoping to catch up on actual work before my mind wandered back to James.

Fat chance of that.

"You're here early," Barb said when she arrived at eight-thirty. "Couldn't sleep?"

"Something like that. Coffee?"

"Please."

I made a pot while she sorted through the morning messages. Normal office routine that felt surreal when my head was still full of monitoring equipment and psychological torture.

"Anything urgent?" I asked, handing her a mug.

"Julie wants to discuss the Patterson account. Sarah called in sick. And. . ." she paused, looking at a pink slip, "someone named Dr. James Wylder called. Said you'd know what it was about?"

My pulse quickened. "I'll call him back."

"New client?"

"Potential consulting arrangement. Psychology research."

Barb nodded and went back to her desk. I closed my office door and dialed James's number.

"Britney! I was hoping to hear from you. What did you think of last night?"

"Fascinating methodology. The level of control you maintain over environmental variables is impressive."

"I'm glad you appreciate the sophistication of our approach. I was wondering - would you be interested in observing another Friday couples session? Different dynamic than what you saw last night."

More intelligence gathering. More time to study his operation.

"That would be valuable. Same time?"

"Seven PM. I think you'll find this particular case quite illuminating. The relationship dynamics under stress are extraordinary."

Extraordinary. Is that what we're calling this?

"I'll be there."

After hanging up, I sat back in my chair and considered my next moves. Three observation sessions would give me a solid understanding of his facility, his methods, his staff. But I needed more than that. I needed to understand his personal routines, his vulnerabilities outside of Nightmares Unleashed.

Time to start the real stalking.

The rest of Wednesday was busy. I handled a staffing crisis for one of our bigger accounts, reviewed contracts for two new placements, and had lunch with a potential client who wanted to expand their temporary workforce.

Regular work stuff that felt increasingly tedious as my mind kept drifting to James.

Thursday morning, I made my decision. I called in sick.

"I think I caught something at that seminar," I told Barb. "Probably be back tomorrow."

"Feel better. I'll handle the Morrison call."

Instead of heading to the office, I drove to USF. James taught a graduate psychology course on Thursday mornings, and I wanted to see him in his natural habitat.

I parked across from Cooper Hall and waited. Students streamed in and out of the building, backpacks slung over shoulders, coffee cups in hand. Young, eager faces that had no idea one of their professors was a monster.

At ten-fifteen, I spotted James walking toward the building. He looked every inch the respected academic - briefcase, pressed shirt, confident stride. He stopped to chat with a colleague near the entrance, laughing at something the other man said.

I followed him inside, keeping my distance. The building was busy enough that one more person wouldn't stand out. I watched him disappear into a classroom, then found a bench in the hallway where I could observe without being obvious.

For the next hour, I listened to the muffled sounds of his lecture through the closed door. Occasionally I caught fragments - something about cognitive behavioral therapy, treatment protocols, ethical considerations.

Ethical considerations. That's rich.

When class ended, students filed out, most of them looking engaged, even excited about what they'd learned. James emerged last, still playing the role of dedicated educator.

I followed him back to his car, noting his route, his timing, his habits. He stopped at the same coffee shop near campus that he'd posted about on social media. Ordered the same drink - large black coffee, no sugar.

Creatures of habit were so much easier to kill.

By Friday afternoon, anticipation was humming through my veins again. Tonight's couples session would be my third observation, and I was starting to get a clear picture of James's operation.

More importantly, I was starting to see the cracks in his facade.

Ready for round three, you twisted piece of shit.

Fifteen

FRIDAY NIGHT'S COUPLES SESSION was everything I'd expected and worse.

James greeted me with his usual enthusiasm, practically vibrating with excitement as he led me to the observation room. Tonight's victims were a young couple in their late twenties - married three years, struggling with intimacy issues after the wife's miscarriage.

"This case perfectly demonstrates the power of shared trauma experiences," James said, adjusting the camera angles. "When couples face their deepest fears together, barriers dissolve."

Barriers dissolve? You mean people break.

The session lasted two and a half hours. I watched James put this grieving couple through scenarios designed to trigger their worst memories, force them to confront their loss in the most brutal ways possible. By the end, they were both sobbing, clinging to each other not out of love but desperation.

"Remarkable breakthrough," James murmured, making notes. "You can see how the controlled environment facilitates emotional vulnerability."

"The insights were remarkable," I managed, fighting the urge to put my knife through his throat right then and there.

I've killed over ten people and this sick fuck still makes my skin crawl.

Walking to my car afterward, I had to grip my keys to keep my hands from shaking. Not from fear - from rage. James had just destroyed two people who'd come to him for help, and he was proud of it.

My phone buzzed as I pulled out of the parking lot.

Thank you for witnessing that session tonight. Your insights about psychological pressure points were particularly astute. I think you're ready for our next phase.

Next phase? I typed back: *What did you have in mind?*

Lunch this week? I'd like to discuss some opportunities for collaboration. Your business acumen combined with my therapeutic methods could be quite profitable.

Profitable. Now we were getting to the real heart of it.

Wednesday works for me.

Perfect. Bern's Steak House, 1 PM. I think you'll find my proposal very interesting.

Saturday morning, I woke up feeling like I'd witnessed something that would haunt me for weeks. Stu was already up, making coffee in the kitchen.

"How was your seminar?" he asked, handing me a mug.

"Disturbing. More disturbing than I expected."

"Want to talk about it?"

I considered how much to tell him. "The presenter is using unethical methods. Claiming it's therapy, but it's really just psychological manipulation for profit."

Stu nodded, stirring sugar into his coffee. "Sounds like James needs to be stopped."

"Yeah. Someone definitely needs to stop him." I wasn't surprised he knew who I meant. Stu always knew.

Saturday was quiet. Stu had to work a half-day, so I spent the morning catching up on laundry and paperwork. When he got home, we grabbed lunch at our favorite Cuban place and walked around Hyde Park. But my mind kept drifting to Wednesday's lunch, to James's "proposal," to how I was going to kill him.

Sunday brought rain and restlessness. I tried to focus on work emails, but kept finding myself researching Bern's Steak House instead. High-end restaurant, private dining rooms available, valet parking. The kind of place where James would feel comfortable discussing business.

The kind of place where he'd let his guard down.

Monday morning, I was in the office early, catching up on actual business before my mind wandered back to murder. Julie called around ten.

"Hey, how was your weekend?"

"Good. Quiet. Yours?"

"Brian had a friend over for a sleepover. I'm exhausted." She laughed. "But speaking of exhausted, you sound tired. Everything okay?"

"Just processing some heavy stuff from that psychology seminar. Really opened my eyes to how manipulative some people can be."

"Yikes. Well, if you need to vent, you know where to find me."

After hanging up, I sat back in my chair and thought about James's text. *Your business acumen combined with my therapeutic methods could be quite profitable.* He wasn't just running a torture operation—he was looking to expand it.

Which meant he was more dangerous than I'd realized.

But it also meant he was getting sloppy. Confident. Ready to bring in a partner he barely knew based on a few observation sessions.

Tuesday crawled by. I handled client calls, reviewed contracts, and tried to act like a normal business owner instead of someone planning murder. Barb noticed my distraction.

"You sure you're feeling okay? You've seemed off all week."

"Just tired. Those psychology seminars are more intense than I expected."

"Maybe take a break from them for a while?"

After Wednesday, I definitely will.

Tuesday night, I lay in bed going over every detail of Wednesday's lunch. Bern's was a busy restaurant, lots of witnesses, not ideal for anything dramatic. But it was perfect for intelligence gathering, for getting James to reveal more about his operation.

The real kill would come later, when I had all the information I needed.

Wednesday morning arrived gray and humid. I dressed carefully - professional but approachable, the kind of outfit that said "successful business woman open to new opportunities." I slipped my knife into its usual place and made sure my phone was fully charged.

Time to find out what you're really after, you twisted piece of shit.

I arrived at Bern's fifteen minutes early and asked for a table in the main dining room. I wanted to see James arrive, watch how he moved through public spaces, note any security habits or nervous tics.

He showed up exactly on time, dressed in an expensive suit, carrying himself with the confidence of someone who owned the world. He spotted me immediately and walked over with that same charming smile I'd seen him use on his victims.

"Britney! You look lovely. Thank you for meeting me."

"My pleasure. I've been curious about this proposal of yours."

Over the next hour and a half, James laid out a plan that made my blood run cold. He wanted to franchise the Nightmares Unleashed concept, create a network of "therapeutic facilities" across the Southeast. He had investors lined up, locations scouted, even government contracts in the works.

"The beauty of your staffing agency," he said, cutting into his steak, "is the access it gives you. Screening potential subjects, identifying psychological vulnerabilities, even recruiting staff for the facilities."

"Subjects," I repeated. "Not clients?"

"Well, yes, technically clients. But let's be honest about what we're really offering here. We're providing experiences that reveal fundamental truths about human nature. The therapeutic benefit is just a useful byproduct."

There it is. The mask comes off.

For the rest of lunch, I listened to James describe his vision for psychological manipulation on an industrial scale. Research contracts with universities. Corporate team-building packages. Even therapeutic programs for prison systems.

By the time dessert arrived, I knew exactly what James Wylder was - and what I had to do about it.

"This all sounds fascinating," I said, stirring my coffee. "But I'd need to see more of your operation before committing to anything this significant."

"Of course. How about next Friday? I can give you a complete tour, show you our research protocols, introduce you to our investors."

"Perfect."

James smiled and signaled for the check. "I have a feeling this is going to be a very profitable partnership."

For one of us.

Driving back to the office, I felt calm for the first time in days. The intelligence gathering was almost complete. One more session, one more chance to study his operation, and then I'd be ready.

James Wylder thought he was recruiting a business partner.

He was actually planning his own funeral.

Sleep tight, you demented piece of shit. Your days are numbered.

Sixteen

THE DAYS UNTIL FRIDAY crawled by like a funeral procession. Every day felt like waiting for Christmas morning, except instead of presents, I was looking forward to a complete tour of James's torture operation.

Thursday brought a surprise call from Joe.

"Hey, kid. Haven't heard from you in a while. How about dinner this weekend? Marsha's been asking about you."

"Sunday work? Stu and I could come over around six."

"Perfect. I'll tell Marsha."

After hanging up, I realized I'd been so focused on James that I'd been neglecting my normal relationships. Joe and Marsha, girls' nights, even some of my regular clients. The obsession was taking over, which meant I needed to be more careful about maintaining my cover.

Friday morning, I made a point of calling three clients to check on their temp placements. Routine maintenance calls that felt increasingly foreign when my mind was consumed with murder.

"Everything's going great with Sarah," the Henderson contact told me. "We'd like to extend her contract through the end of next month."

"Wonderful. I'll have the paperwork ready Monday."

These were the kinds of calls that used to energize me. Building relationships, expanding contracts, growing the business. Now they felt like distractions from more important work.

Around lunch, my phone buzzed with a message from James.

Looking forward to tonight. I think you'll find our research protocols particularly enlightening. Fair warning - some of what you'll see might challenge conventional therapeutic boundaries.

I'm prepared for anything.

Good. That's exactly the mindset our partnership will require.

Partnership. He was already thinking of me as a business partner, someone who shared his vision. The arrogance was staggering.

But it was also useful. Arrogant people made mistakes.

I left the office early, claiming I had a doctor's appointment. Barb barely looked up from her computer.

"Hope everything's okay," she said, looking up with concern. "You've been running to a lot of appointments lately."

"Just some follow-up stuff. Nothing serious."

At home, I changed into my usual reconnaissance outfit and checked that my knife was secure. Tonight wasn't about violence—it was about intelligence. But I never went anywhere unarmed.

Stu was already at work, pulling another double shift. I'd texted him earlier about tonight's "seminar," and he'd responded with his usual supportive message: *Learn everything you can. Love you.*

The drive to Nightmares Unleashed felt different this time. Less nervous energy, more cold calculation. I knew the building, the layout, the security measures. Tonight was about seeing the bigger picture.

James was waiting for me in the lobby, dressed in expensive casual clothes - polo shirt, khakis, leather shoes that probably cost more than most people made in a week.

"Britney! Right on time. Tonight's going to be special."

"I'm sure," I said dryly.

He led me down a hallway I hadn't seen before, past the observation rooms to what looked like executive offices. The décor was sleek and modern, all glass and chrome, with the kind of minimalist design that screamed money.

"Before we begin the tour," James said, opening a door marked "Conference Room A," "I'd like you to meet some of the key players in our organization."

Inside the conference room, three people sat around a polished table. Two men in expensive suits, one woman in a tailored blazer. They all had the same predatory look in their eyes that I'd seen in James.

"Gentlemen, Dr. Martinez, I'd like you to meet Britney Cage. The business owner I've been telling you about."

The introductions were a blur of fake smiles and firm handshakes. Dr. Martinez was the woman I'd seen conducting intake sessions. The two men - Dr. Richardson and someone named Mr. Vance - were apparently investors and research partners.

"James tells us you're interested in psychological applications for workforce management," Dr. Richardson said. "Our methodologies have shown remarkable results in breaking down resistance patterns."

Breaking down resistance patterns? Jesus Christ.

"It's a fascinating field," I said carefully. "I'd love to understand more about your research protocols."

For the next hour, I sat through the most disturbing business presentation I'd ever witnessed. They laid out their expansion plans with PowerPoint slides and profit projections. Franchising opportunities. Government contracts. Corporate partnerships.

They weren't just running one torture facility—they were building an empire.

"The beauty of your staffing agency," Mr. Vance said, "is the screening opportunities it provides. We could identify ideal subjects through your placement interviews, assess psychological vulnerabilities, even recruit subjects directly."

Subjects. Always subjects, never people.

"Our research indicates that certain personality types respond particularly well to intensive therapeutic intervention," Dr. Martinez added. "Trauma survivors, individuals with authority issues, people struggling with relationship dynamics."

They were talking about targeting the most vulnerable people in society, the ones who needed actual help, and turning them into research subjects for psychological torture.

"This is impressive," I managed, fighting every instinct to put my knife through the nearest throat. "What would my role be in this partnership?"

James leaned forward, eyes bright with excitement. "Subject identification and recruitment through your agency. Staff screening for our facilities. And eventually, direct participation in research protocols."

"Direct participation?"

"We're developing couples therapy programs that require business partnerships as case studies. Successful professional relationships under con-

trolled stress environments. You and your partner would be ideal subjects."

*He wants to torture Stu and me as a fucking
research project.*

"That sounds. . . intense," I said.

"Intensity is where breakthrough occurs," Dr.
Richardson said. "We've learned that conventional therapeutic boundaries actually prevent
genuine psychological progress."

They showed me more slides. Research data
that looked legitimate but was clearly fabricated.
Financial projections that made my skin crawl.
Photos of facilities they were planning to build
across Florida, Georgia, and Alabama.

By the time the presentation ended, I understood exactly what I was dealing with. This
wasn't just one sick individual with a psychology degree. This was an organized operation with
serious backing and expansion plans.

Which meant killing James wouldn't be
enough. They'd just replace him with someone
else.

But it also meant they were creating a paper
trail. Financial records, research protocols, in-
vestor communications. All the evidence needed
to bring down the entire operation.

"So what do you think?" James asked as the
others filed out of the conference room. "Ready
to be part of something revolutionary?"

"I need to see the facility in operation first," I said. "Tonight's tour will help me understand the scope of what you're proposing."

"Of course. I think you'll be very impressed with our methodologies."

The tour that followed was worse than I'd imagined. James showed me rooms I hadn't seen before - sensory deprivation chambers, interrogation-style interview rooms, even what looked like medical examination tables with restraints.

"We're expanding into physiological research," he explained. "Measuring stress responses, brain activity patterns, hormone levels during intensive therapeutic sessions."

They're experimenting on people like lab rats.

In one room, a session was in progress. Through the one-way glass, I watched a woman in her forties being subjected to what James called "controlled panic induction." She was restrained in a chair, wearing headphones and a VR headset, clearly in distress.

"This subject suffers from claustrophobia," James said, adjusting controls on a nearby panel. "We're exposing her to increasingly confined virtual environments while monitoring her physiological responses."

The woman was sobbing, pulling against her restraints, begging to be released. James ignored her completely, focused on the readouts on his screens.

This is the most evil thing I've ever seen.

"Remarkable stress response patterns," he murmured, making notes. "This data will be invaluable for our research."

I watched for another few minutes, memorizing every detail. The equipment, the security measures, the staff protocols. When we finally left, I felt like I needed a shower.

"What did you think?" James asked as we headed back to the lobby.

"Remarkable," I said, the word tasting like poison. "Your research protocols are unlike anything I've encountered."

"I'm glad you appreciate the sophistication of our methods. So, are you ready to discuss partnership terms?"

"I'd like to review everything we talked about tonight. When can we meet again?"

"How about lunch next week? We can discuss the specifics of your involvement."

"Perfect."

James walked me to my car, still talking about expansion plans and research opportunities. I nodded at appropriate moments, made interested sounds, played the role of potential business partner.

But inside, I was calculating. James wasn't just a monster—he was part of something bigger and more dangerous than I'd realized.

Which meant I needed to be smarter about how I handled this.

Driving home, I felt that familiar calm wash over me. Not the anticipation of a simple kill, but the satisfaction of a puzzle finally coming together.

James Wylder and his associates thought they were building an empire of psychological torture.

They had no idea they were constructing their own elaborate tomb.

Sleep well tonight, you sadistic bastards. You're going to need your rest.

Seventeen

Saturday morning, I woke up with murder on my mind.

Not unusual for me, but this felt different. More focused. I'd been thinking about James's operation all night, turning over details, analyzing weaknesses.

The scope of what I'd seen Friday night was staggering. This wasn't just one sick individual—it was an organized network with serious backing. But that also meant more opportunities. More ways to destroy them.

Stu was already up, making coffee in the kitchen. He handed me a mug without a word, reading my mood.

"Rough night?" he asked.

"Productive night. That seminar was more enlightening than I expected."

"Want to talk about it?"

I set my mug down and leaned against the counter. "Remember that couple I told you about? The ones who tried to leave?"

"Yeah."

"It wasn't just them. There are others. A whole network of people doing this shit."

Stu's expression darkened. "How many others?"

"Investors, researchers, expansion plans across three states. This isn't some amateur operation."

"What are you thinking?"

"I'm thinking James isn't the only problem. But he's the one I can reach."

We stood there in comfortable silence, both understanding what that meant. Stu had never questioned my methods, never asked me to justify what I did. He got it.

"Need help with anything?" he asked.

"Just keep being you. When this is over, I want to come home to something normal."

Around noon, Julie called.

"Hey, want to grab lunch? Cody and Brian are having a boys day, so I'm free for a few hours."

"Perfect. Meet at that Cuban place in Hyde Park?"

"See you there in twenty."

Lunch with Julie was exactly what I needed - normal conversation that had nothing to do with psychological torture or murder. She was excited about a new client prospect, worried about Brian's upcoming science fair project, and happy that Cody had finally gotten a promotion at work.

"You seem different," she said over dessert. "More relaxed than you've been in weeks."

"I figured out how to handle that work situation I was dealing with."

"Good. You were getting a little intense there for a while."

* * *

Sunday brought the dinner at Joe's I'd promised. Stu and I arrived right on time, bearing wine and flowers for Marsha.

"There's my favorite girl," Joe said, wrapping me in one of his bear hugs. "How have you been, kid?"

"Good. Busy, but good."

Marsha appeared from the kitchen, looking pleased to see us. "Britney! I was hoping you'd be able to make it."

She was wearing one of her flowing dresses, the kind that made her look like she'd stepped out of a 1970s commune. Her dark hair was pulled back in a loose bun, and she had that serene smile she always wore when she was trying too hard to seem zen.

"Sorry it's been so long," I said, handing her the flowers. "Work's been crazy."

"These are beautiful. Thank you." She buried her face in the bouquet. "Gardenias. My favorite."

I hadn't known that, but I nodded anyway.

Joe was already manning the grill on the back patio, beer in hand, looking more relaxed than I'd seen him in months.

"Stu! Come grab a beer and tell me about this boat situation."

While the men talked boating and boat maintenance, Marsha and I went into the kitchen. She'd made enough food to feed a small army - salad, rice, black beans, plantains, and some kind of sauce that smelled incredible.

"You've outdone yourself," I said.

"I like having people to cook for." She handed me a glass of wine. "Joe's been eating nothing but sandwiches and cereal since I've been traveling so much."

"Where did you go this time?"

"Costa Rica. There's a retreat center there that does amazing work with trauma recovery. Melissa and I are thinking about going back next year."

"Sounds interesting."

"It really is. They use natural settings and community support instead of traditional therapy. Much more holistic."

I sipped my wine and let her talk about healing crystals and energy work while I prepped the salad. Marsha meant well, but her new-age approach to everything grated on me sometimes. She saw the world as this place where everyone could be healed with enough positive thinking and organic vegetables.

She had no idea what real darkness looked like.

"You seem tense," she said, studying my face. "Are you taking care of yourself?"

"I'm fine, Marsha. Just tired."

"Have you tried meditation? I could teach you some breathing exercises."

"Thanks, but I'm good."

She didn't push, but I could feel her watching me as we finished preparing dinner. Marsha had always been too perceptive for her own good.

When we moved to the patio, Joe was in full storytelling mode, describing his latest golf round to Stu with dramatic hand gestures.

"So there I am, on the back nine, and this shot that should have been a simple approach ends up in the water hazard. My ball just disappears!"

Stu was laughing, completely drawn into the story. It was nice seeing him relaxed. His job was stressful enough without having to worry about my extracurricular activities.

"Did you make the shot?" I asked, settling into the chair next to him.

"Hell yes, I made it. Took three more strokes, but I got it on the green." Joe grinned. "Marsha said I should have just taken the penalty stroke, but where's the fun in that?"

We ate on the patio as the sun started to set, the conversation flowing between work gossip, local news, and Joe's golf schedule. Marsha kept the wine flowing, and by the time we got to dessert, everyone was pleasantly buzzed.

"This chicken is incredible, Marsha," Stu said, finishing his plate.

"Thank you. It's my grandmother's recipe."

"Best round I've had in months," Joe said proudly. "Marsha wanted me to take the penalty stroke, said the smart play was the right play."

"My point was valid," Marsha said firmly. "Sometimes the smart play is the right play."

"Good thing you didn't listen to her," I said. "That was some great golf."

Joe beamed. "Anyway, Marsha's got magic hands in the kitchen."

Marsha blushed at the compliment. "I just follow the recipes my grandmother taught me."

"Your grandmother was Cuban?" Stu asked.

"Half Cuban, half Italian. She could make anything taste good."

The conversation drifted to family stories, travel plans, and Joe's latest doctor visits. He was doing well for his age, but I could see the subtle changes. Moving a little slower, needing more rest. It made me appreciate these dinners more.

"You've been quiet tonight," Marsha observed as we cleared the table. "Everything okay?"

"Yeah, work's been intense lately."

"You work too hard," Joe said. "Need to learn to delegate."

"That's what Barb keeps telling me."

"Smart woman, that Barb. You should listen to her."

We moved inside for coffee and dessert - flan that Marsha had made from scratch. Joe insisted on showing Stu his latest golf clubs while Marsha and I cleaned up in the kitchen.

"He really enjoys having you two here," she said quietly. "He talks about you all the time. How proud he is of what you've built."

I felt that familiar twist of guilt. Joe had no idea what I'd really built, what I was really capable of. To him, I was just his successful surrogate daughter who ran a staffing agency.

"He's been good to me," I said.

"You've been good to him too. Especially after his heart attack. You were there every day."

I remembered those weeks in the hospital, sitting by Joe's bed while he recovered from surgery. The fear that I might lose the closest thing to a father I'd ever had.

"Of course I was there."

"Not everyone would have been. You could have just sent flowers and visited once or twice. But you were there."

We finished cleaning up in comfortable silence. Through the kitchen window, I could see Joe and Stu on the back patio, Joe gesturing enthusiastically while describing some golf technique.

"They get along well," Marsha said, following my gaze.

"Joe likes him."

"Joe loves him. Says he's never seen you this happy."

That's because he doesn't know who--what--I really am.

By the time we left, it was almost ten. Stu and I drove home in comfortable silence, both of us processing the evening.

"Good dinner," he said finally.

"Marsha outdid herself."

"Joe seems to be doing well."

"Yeah. Better than I expected."

Back home, we got ready for bed without talking much. I was tired, but my mind was already shifting back to Monday, to James, to the work I still had to do.

"You okay?" Stu asked as we settled into bed.

"Just thinking about Joe. Getting older, you know?"

"He's tough. He'll be around for a long time."

"I hope so."

"You sure that's all?"

I turned to face him in the dark. "Sometimes I wonder what he'd think if he knew who I really was."

"He knows who you are. You're the woman who sat by his hospital bed every day. You're the daughter he never had."

"But if he knew about the other stuff—"

"He'd still love you. Joe's not stupid, Brit. He knows you're not perfect. None of us are."

As Stu fell asleep beside me, I stared at the ceiling and thought about normal things. Family dinners and golf stories and the kind of love that didn't require hiding bodies.

Tomorrow I'd go back to planning murder. But tonight, I could pretend to be the kind of person who deserved Joe's pride.

The kind of person who deserved this family.

Tomorrow I'd start the real work.

Eighteen

Monday morning arrived with the kind of crisp focus I hadn't felt in weeks. Stu left for his early shift with a quick kiss and his usual "be careful" - words that meant more now that he knew what I was really planning.

I made my coffee, fed Minion, and sat at the kitchen table with my laptop. Time to get serious about James Wylder.

First things first - I needed to map out his routines without leaving digital footprints. I drove to a different coffee shop across town, paid cash, and used their Wi-Fi on the burner laptop I kept for exactly these situations.

James's social media told a story of predictable habits. Morning runs along Bayshore Boulevard at 6 AM. Same coffee shop near campus afterward. Office hours at USF on Wednesdays and Fridays. Faculty meetings on Thursday afternoons.

But it was his personal posts that gave me the real intel. Photos from the same gym downtown - Iron Temple on Kennedy. Check-ins at Bern's Steak House for what looked like regular business dinners. Always alone or with other professionals, never anyone who looked personal.

No girlfriend. No close friends. Just work contacts and business associates.

Perfect.

I spent two hours building a timeline of his public activities, then drove to the office. Barb was already there, efficiently sorting through the morning chaos.

"You look focused today," she said, handing me my messages.

"Slept well for once. What's the damage?"

"Three callbacks, two new inquiries, and Julie wants to discuss one of the new client prospects."

I settled into my office and forced myself to handle legitimate business for a few hours. Called clients, reviewed contracts, approved placements. The mundane work of running a staffing agency felt surreal when my mind was already planning murder.

Around noon, I called Julie back about the client prospect.

"Marketing firm downtown," she said. "They need three temps for a product launch next month."

"What kind of positions?"

"Administrative support, data entry, and someone with social media experience."

We spent ten minutes working out the details. Normal business that used to energize me. Now it felt like marking time until I could get back to the real work.

By one o'clock, I was back in my car, heading to scope out James's neighborhood. He lived in Hyde Park, in one of those renovated bungalows that screamed "successful academic." Nice street, minimal privacy between houses, decent foot traffic from joggers and dog walkers.

I parked two blocks away and walked past his house like I belonged there. Tidy front yard, security system sign, BMW in the driveway. A few windows with blinds drawn, but I could see into the kitchen and what looked like a home office.

Too exposed for anything dramatic during daylight hours. But useful intel for later.

I drove past Iron Temple next. Small parking lot, single entrance, busy enough that one more person wouldn't stand out. James's BMW wasn't there, which meant he probably worked out in the mornings before his run.

The coffee shop near campus was my next stop. I bought a latte and sat in the corner, watching the flow of customers. Mostly students and faculty, predictable patterns, easy to blend in. James's usual spot appeared to be a table near the window where he could people-watch while drinking his black coffee.

The problem was obvious - James knew what I looked like, and he'd definitely remember my Jeep from the Nightmares Unleashed sessions. I'd have to be smarter about this. Maybe borrow Stu's car for the real surveillance work, change my appearance when I could.

By three, I was back at the office, slipping back into my normal routine.

"How was your lunch?" Barb asked.

"Relaxing."

The rest of the afternoon crawled by. I handled client calls, reviewed invoices, and tried to look busy while my mind stayed focused on James. By five, I was ready to start the real surveillance.

I changed clothes in the office bathroom - dark jeans, black hoodie, baseball cap. Nothing that would stand out but enough to alter my appearance if anyone noticed me. I slipped my knife into its usual place and checked that my phone was fully charged.

Time to see where James Wylder went when he thought no one was watching.

His house was quiet when I drove past at six. BMW still in the driveway, lights on in what looked like the kitchen. I parked three blocks away and walked back, finding a spot behind a neighbor's hedge where I could watch his front door without being obvious.

At 6:45, the front door opened. James emerged wearing workout clothes and carrying a gym bag. He loaded the bag into his BMW and backed out of the driveway, heading toward downtown.

I followed at a distance, keeping two cars between us. He drove straight to Iron Temple, just like his social media suggested. I parked across the street and settled in to wait.

For the next hour and a half, I watched the gym entrance. A few people went in and out, but mostly it was quiet. Professional types getting their evening workout, nothing unusual.

At 8:20, James emerged looking satisfied and slightly sweaty. He loaded his gym bag and drove straight home, no stops.

I followed him back to Hyde Park and resumed my position behind the hedge. Lights came on in different rooms as he moved through the house - kitchen, living room, what looked like his home office. Normal evening routine.

By ten, the house was mostly dark except for one upstairs window. Bedroom, probably. James Wylder was settling in for the night, completely unaware that someone was cataloging his every move.

I walked back to my car feeling satisfied. Day one of surveillance complete. Nothing dramatic, but I was building a picture of his habits, his vulnerabilities.

Tomorrow I'd follow him during his morning routine. See if he was as predictable as his social media suggested.

As I drove home, I thought about Stu's words from the night before. Joe knew I wasn't perfect, and he loved me anyway. But Joe had no idea what "not perfect" really meant in my case.

James Wylder was about to find out exactly how imperfect I could be.

The house was dark when I got home. Stu was working another late shift, probably wouldn't be back until after midnight. I fed Minion, heated up leftover Chinese takeout, and settled on the couch with my laptop.

Time to do some deeper research on Dr. James Wylder.

I started with academic databases, looking for his published research. Most of it was standard psychology stuff - trauma response, behavioral modification, exposure therapy techniques. But buried in the citations was a pattern that made my stomach turn.

References to "enhanced interrogation techniques." Studies on "psychological pressure points" funded by government contractors. Research into "breaking resistant subjects."

James hadn't just stumbled into psychological torture for profit. He'd been training for it his entire career.

The more I dug, the angrier I got. This wasn't some desperate academic looking for extra income. This was a predator who'd spent years learning how to break people systematically, then created Nightmares Unleashed as his personal laboratory.

My phone buzzed with a text from Stu: *Working late. Don't wait up. Love you.*

I texted back: *Love you too. Be safe.*

Then I went back to my research, building a comprehensive picture of James Wylder's sick little empire. By the time I finally went to bed at midnight, I had enough information to plan his death ten different ways.

But I only needed one.

Nineteen

Tuesday morning I woke up before my alarm, adrenaline already coursing through my veins. Today I'd follow James through his morning routine - assuming he was as predictable as his social media suggested.

Stu was already gone. Another early shift, another day of him pretending not to know what I was really doing while I was "at work." I grabbed coffee and a protein bar, then headed out to swap vehicles with him at the station parking lot. We'd worked this out the night before - he'd take my Jeep to work, I'd take his car.

His black Dodge Charger was perfect for surveillance. Tinted windows, unremarkable enough that James wouldn't notice it, and definitely not connected to me in his mind.

By 5:45 AM, I was parked two blocks from James's house with a clear view of his driveway. The street was quiet except for a few early joggers and someone walking their dog. Perfect cover.

At exactly 6:02, James's front door opened. He emerged in running gear, did a few quick stretches on his front porch, then took off down the street at a steady pace.

I gave him a thirty-second head start, then followed in the car. He ran the same route I'd mapped from his social media posts - down Bayshore Boulevard, along the water, then back through Hyde Park. Forty-three minutes, almost to the second.

Back at his house, he disappeared inside for twenty minutes. Shower, probably. Then he emerged again, this time dressed for work and carrying a travel mug and briefcase.

First stop: the coffee shop near campus. He parked, went inside, came out eight minutes later with what looked like a second coffee and a pastry. Same table by the window, same routine I'd observed yesterday.

I parked across the street and watched him through the window. He pulled out his phone, scrolled through something - probably email or social media. Took a few sips of coffee, ate half the pastry, checked his watch.

Boring as hell. But useful.

At 7:45, he packed up and drove to USF. I followed him to the faculty parking lot, then peeled off. No point in pushing my luck on campus where security cameras were everywhere.

Instead, I drove back to my office. Time to maintain the illusion that I was actually running a business.

Barb was opening up when I arrived.

"You're here early," she said, looking surprised.

"Couldn't sleep. Figured I'd get a head start on the day."

"Coffee's not ready yet, but I can make some."

"I'm good. Maybe later."

I settled into my office and actually did some work. Reviewed the marketing firm's requirements, pulled candidate files, made notes about who might be a good fit. The kind of legitimate business activity that kept the money flowing and the IRS happy.

Around ten, Julie called with an update on another placement.

"The law firm loves Marcus," she said. "They want to extend him through the end of next month."

"Perfect. He's working out well for them."

"Yeah, and it means steady income for him while he studies for the bar exam."

We talked through a few more placements, scheduled some interviews, covered the usual Tuesday business. Normal stuff that felt increasingly disconnected from what I really cared about.

By noon, I was ready to continue surveillance. I told Barb I had client meetings for the afternoon and would probably work from home tomorrow.

"Sounds good," she said. "I'll handle things here."

I spent the afternoon tracking James's movements again. Faculty meeting at 2 PM - I watched him walk into the psychology building with three other professors. They emerged ninety minutes later, James looking slightly annoyed. Politics, probably.

Then back to his office for two hours. I couldn't see what he was doing, but lights were on and I occasionally saw his silhouette moving around.

At 5:30, he packed up and left campus. I expected him to head home, but instead he drove to a restaurant downtown. Upscale place, valet parking, the kind of spot where academics took potential donors or important colleagues.

I parked across the street and watched through the restaurant's front windows. James sat at a table with two people I didn't recognize - a woman in her fifties wearing expensive jewelry and a younger man in a suit. Business dinner, from the look of it.

They talked for two hours. I couldn't hear anything, obviously, but their body language was interesting. The woman did most of the talking, gesturing enthusiastically. James nodded a lot, occasionally pulling out his phone to show them something. The younger man took notes.

Investors, maybe. Or potential partners for expanding Nightmares Unleashed.

By the time they finished dinner, it was almost eight. James shook hands with both of them, looking pleased. Whatever they'd discussed had gone well.

He drove straight home after that. Lights came on in his kitchen, then his living room, finally his upstairs office. Working late, probably following up on whatever had been discussed at dinner.

I gave it another hour, then called it a night. Two days of surveillance complete, and James's patterns were becoming clear. He was a creature of habit, which would make planning his death much easier.

The trick would be finding the right moment when he was vulnerable and isolated. His house was too exposed, his campus office too risky. But there had to be something.

There always was.

* * *

Wednesday morning brought rain, which complicated surveillance but provided good cover. I was back in Stu's car by 5:45, watching James's house through the steady drizzle.

His routine didn't change much. Still went for his run, though he cut it short because of the weather. Still hit the coffee shop, though he sat inside longer since the patio was wet.

But something was different about his demeanor. He seemed more animated, checking his phone more frequently, even taking a call while he was at the coffee shop. Whatever had happened at dinner last night had energized him.

At USF, instead of heading to his usual office, he went to what looked like an administrative building. Stayed there for three hours, coming out with a thick folder and a satisfied expression.

Paperwork. Permits, maybe, or funding applications. The kind of bureaucratic stuff you'd need to expand a business operation.

The pieces were starting to fit together. James wasn't just running Nightmares Unleashed as a side project. He was building something bigger, and last night's dinner had been a major step forward.

Which meant I needed to move faster than I'd planned.

By the time I got home that evening, I had the beginnings of a plan. Not the full execution yet, but a framework. Something that would take advantage of James's predictable habits while minimizing my exposure.

Stu was already home, looking tired after another long shift.

"How was your day?" he asked, settling onto the couch beside me.

"Productive. I'm getting a clearer picture of the situation."

"Good. Any timeline?"

"Soon. Next week, probably. I've got another couples session to observe Saturday - that might be the perfect opportunity. Use the facility itself."

He nodded, understanding what I meant without me having to spell it out. Another reason I loved him - he got the operational side of what I did without needing all the details.

"Need anything from me?"

"Actually, yeah. I need you inside, watching the cameras and security feeds while I work. Think you can handle that?"

He pulled me against his side. "You're good at this, Brit. Trust your instincts."

I did trust my instincts. And my instincts were telling me that James Wylder had maybe a week left to live.

Twenty

Thursday morning I skipped the surveillance routine. Three days of watching James had given me enough intel about his patterns. Now I needed to focus on the facility itself.

I drove to Nightmares Unleashed in my Jeep, parking in the visitor section like any other potential client. During business hours, the place looked completely different - cleaner, more professional, almost legitimate. But I knew what happened here after dark.

A receptionist I didn't recognize sat behind the front desk, typing something on her computer. Young, probably a college student working part-time. She looked up when I walked in.

"Can I help you?"

"I'm here about scheduling another observation session," I said. "I've been working with Dr. Wylder on some research."

She checked her computer screen. "What's your name?"

"Britney Cage."

"Oh yes, I see you here. Let me call Dr. Wylder."

She picked up the phone and spoke quietly for a moment, then hung up.

"He'll be right out."

I used the wait time to study the lobby layout. Two exits - the main door I'd come through and what looked like a side door marked "Emergency Exit Only." Security cameras in three corners, probably more throughout the building. A keypad next to the door leading to the back areas.

"Britney!" James emerged from the back, looking pleased to see me. "I wasn't expecting you today."

"I was in the area and thought I'd stop by. I've been thinking about Saturday's session."

"Excellent. Come back to my office and we can discuss the details."

He led me down the same hallway I'd walked before, past the observation rooms to his office. It was exactly what I'd expected from an academic - books everywhere, diplomas on the walls, a coffee mug that said "World's Greatest Psychology Professor."

"Please, sit," he said, settling behind his desk. "I'm excited about Saturday's session. The couple we're working with presents some fascinating dynamics."

"What's their situation?"

"Married twelve years, two children. They've been struggling since the husband lost his job six months ago. Traditional therapy wasn't helping them process the trauma of financial instability."

Of course it wasn't helping. Because they probably needed actual support, not psychological torture disguised as therapy.

"And your approach?"

"We'll put them through scenarios that replicate and amplify their current stressors. Financial pressure, threat of losing their home, children at risk. When they're forced to confront their worst fears together, the breakthrough is remarkable."

I nodded like this made perfect sense instead of making me want to put my knife through his heart.

"The session starts at eight?" I asked.

"Yes. You're welcome to observe from the control room again. I think you'll find this even more instructive than the previous sessions."

We talked for another twenty minutes about his "methodology" and the "research applications" for my business. I played the part of the interested potential partner while mentally cataloging every detail of his office, the building layout, the security measures I could see.

When I left, I had a much clearer picture of how Saturday would work. James would be focused on his victims, completely absorbed in the twisted psychology of breaking them down. He'd never see me coming.

* * *

Friday passed in a blur. I handled client calls, reviewed placements, and tried to act like someone whose biggest concern was temp staffing instead of murder. Julie stopped by around lunch with sandwiches from our favorite deli, and I found myself struggling to focus on her stories about Brian's latest school project.

"You seem distracted," she said, looking at me with concern. "Everything okay?"

"Just tired. Been working too many long days."

"Maybe you should take a vacation after this busy period is over."

"Maybe I will."

After she left, I sat in my office and thought about what came after Saturday. James would be dead, his sick operation would collapse, and I'd go back to being just another business owner in Tampa. The thought should have been comforting, but instead it felt hollow.

I'd gotten used to having a purpose beyond profit and loss statements. Used to the clarity that came with hunting someone who deserved to die. When this was over, what would fill that void?

But that was a problem for next week. Right now, I had a kill to plan.

That evening, Stu and I went over the details one more time. I drew him a rough map of the facility layout, showed him where the security cameras were positioned, explained how the observation room controls worked.

"Your job is to watch the monitors and make sure no one surprises us," I said. "James will be completely focused on the session, but there might be other staff around."

"What about the couple? The victims?"

"They'll be traumatized and confused. I'll inject James with ketamine while he's focused on the session, then wait for the couple to finish and leave. Once they're gone, we secure him to one of his own tables and finish what he started."

"And after?"

"The usual," I said. "Good thing we finally got that boat."

Stu smiled grimly. "Told you it would come in handy."

Stu nodded, understanding the plan without needing every detail spelled out. He'd done this kind of thing before in different contexts - the operational mindset was the same whether you were planning a police raid or a murder.

"One more thing," I said. "Bring your service weapon. Just in case."

"You expecting trouble?"

"No. But I like backup plans."

"What about the ketamine?"

"Already have it."

Saturday couldn't come fast enough. I'd been planning this kill for weeks, building up to the moment when I'd finally make James Wylder pay for what he was doing to innocent people. The anticipation was almost unbearable.

But first, I had to get through one more day of pretending to be normal.

Twenty-One

FRIDAY DRAGGED ON ENDLESSLY. Every minute felt like an hour, every task an eternity. I was chomping at the bit, adrenaline coursing under my skin with nowhere to go.

I tried to focus on work, but my mind kept drifting to tomorrow night. To James's face when he realized what was happening. To the moment when I'd finally make him pay for every person he'd broken in the name of research.

Around three, my phone buzzed with a group text from Julie.

Girls' night tonight! The Pub at 7:30. Who's in?

I'm in! Sarah replied immediately.

Can't wait! from Barb.

See you there, I typed back, though the idea of sitting through dinner and drinks felt impossible. But canceling would raise questions I didn't want to answer.

Since Barb was coming to girls' night too, we both left early. I went home to kill time. Cleaned my knife, checked my supplies, went over the plan one more time in my head. Stu wouldn't be home until late - another double shift.

By the time I got to The Pub, the others were already there. Julie waved me over to our usual table, looking more relaxed than I'd seen her in weeks.

"Finally!" she said as I sat down. "I was starting to think you'd forgotten about us."

"Never. Just been crazy busy lately."

Sarah launched into a story about her thesis defense, how nervous she was, how her advisor kept changing the requirements. Barb talked about Jim and how he'd surprised her with dinner at some fancy restaurant downtown. Julie complained about Brian's latest obsession with skateboarding and how she was terrified he'd break his neck.

Normal friend conversations. Normal lives with normal problems.

I nodded and smiled and made appropriate responses, but inside I was vibrating with anticipation. Tomorrow night, I'd be watching James die. Tomorrow night, I'd finally have justice for every victim he'd tortured.

"You're quiet tonight," Julie observed over dessert. "Everything okay?"

"Just tired. Long week."

"You've been saying that a lot lately."

Because I've been planning a murder, but thanks for noticing.

"Things have been intense. I'll be better after this weekend."

That was true enough. After tomorrow, everything would be different.

Sarah ordered another round of wine, and the conversation shifted to weekend plans. Julie was taking Brian to some science museum. Barb and Jim were going antiquing. Normal Saturday activities for normal people.

"What about you, Brit?" Sarah asked. "Any fun plans?"

"Nothing special. Probably just stay in, catch up on some reading."

Good thing I could act. The lie rolled off my tongue effortlessly, no hint of what I was really planning. None of them suspected that their friend was a serial killer, that I'd spent the week stalking my next victim, that tomorrow night I'd be elbow-deep in blood.

We stayed at The Pub until almost ten. By the time I got home, I was exhausted from maintaining the facade. Stu's car wasn't in the driveway - still working his double shift.

I fed Minion, poured a glass of wine, and sat on the couch trying to relax. But my mind wouldn't stop racing. Tomorrow. Tomorrow. Tomorrow.

I went to bed early but couldn't sleep. Every time I closed my eyes, I saw James's face. Heard his voice describing his "methodology." Felt the rage building in my chest like a living thing.

At 3 AM, I gave up and went downstairs. Made coffee, sat at the kitchen table, and went over the plan one more time. Every detail, every contingency, every possible complication.

Stu found me there when he got home at four.

"Couldn't sleep?" he asked, settling into the chair across from me.

"Too wired."

"It's normal. Big day tomorrow."

He poured himself coffee and we sat in comfortable silence. Outside, the world was dark and quiet. In a few hours, the sun would rise on my last day of preparation.

"You ready?" he asked.

"I've been ready for weeks."

"Good. Get some rest. You'll need it."

I nodded, knowing he was right. Tomorrow would be physically and emotionally draining. I needed to be sharp, focused, completely in control.

But first, I had to get through Saturday. One more day of pretending to be normal while inside I counted down the hours until James Wylder's death.

Saturday morning I woke up feeling calm and focused. Today was the day James Wylder would finally understand what real fear felt like.

I made coffee, fed Minion, and went through my usual weekend routine. Laundry, grocery shopping, cleaning the house. Domestic activities that helped maintain the illusion of a peaceful Saturday.

Stu called in sick for his evening shift around noon, giving him the perfect alibi for being unavailable during the time of James's death. We spent the afternoon together, acting like any normal Saturday.

The hours passed slowly. I tried reading, watching TV, doing anything to keep my mind occupied. But all I could think about was tonight. About justice. About finally making James pay.

By six PM, I was ready. I grabbed my bag from the closet and double-checked the contents one more time. Everything I needed was there—duct tape, ketamine already loaded in a syringe, zip ties, plastic sheeting, rubber gloves. I added my knife and phone to the collection.

At the door, I turned back to look at the house Stu and I had made into a home. The living room where we watched movies, the kitchen where we cooked together, the bedroom where we'd built something real and good. After tonight, I'd come back here, and James Wylder would never hurt anyone again.

I drove to the facility in my Jeep. A calculated risk—I could have taken Stu's car or used a rental, but tonight I wanted this to be personal. Let James see Britney Cage, successful business owner, walking through his door. Let him understand that sometimes the monsters you create come back to destroy you.

The Nightmares Unleashed parking lot was almost empty except for James's BMW and one other car. A staff vehicle, probably. I parked two spaces away from his car—close enough to send a message, far enough to avoid suspicion.

Walking to the main entrance, my bag heavy with the tools of justice, I felt that familiar calm settle over me. The building looked different at night—less like a modern office complex, more like what it really was. A house of horrors dressed up in professional lighting and contemporary architecture.

The security guard looked up as I entered. Young, probably college-aged, working his way through school. Another innocent person caught in James's web.

"Ms. Cage? I wasn't expecting anyone tonight."

The same kid from the preview night. I remembered his nervous smile, the way he'd seemed overwhelmed by the crowd of wealthy donors and business leaders.

"Dr. Wylder and I have a private session scheduled," I said, offering my warmest smile. "He should be expecting me."

The guard checked his computer, frowning slightly. "I don't see anything on the schedule . . ."

"Oh, this was arranged last minute. You know how these academics are—always thinking of new research opportunities." I leaned against his desk conspiratorially. "Between you and me, I think he's hoping to land a major corporate contract with my staffing agency."

That seemed to satisfy him. Money talked in every language, and the promise of corporate contracts was something everyone understood.

He buzzed me through the inner door. "Dr. Wylder should be in his office. Down the hall, last door on the right."

"Thanks, sweetie."

I walked down the corridor I'd toured just days ago, past the room where I'd watched that poor woman being tortured, past the domestic violence scenario that had made my skin crawl. The hallway felt longer at night, more oppressive, like the walls were closing in.

Soon all of this will be over.

Time to finish what I'd started.

Twenty-Two

THE HALLWAY FELT DIFFERENT at night. Sterile white walls and modern lighting that looked professional during the day now seemed cold and clinical, like a hospital where no one got better.

James's office door was closed, but I could see light underneath and hear the soft sound of classical music playing inside. Working late, just like his social media had suggested he did most Saturday nights.

I knocked softly.

"Come in."

James looked up from his computer as I entered, his face lighting up with surprise and pleasure. He was dressed casually—jeans and a polo shirt instead of his usual business attire. More relaxed. More vulnerable.

"Britney! This is unexpected. I thought we were meeting next week to discuss the partnership terms."

"I've been thinking about our conversation," I said, closing the door behind me and engaging the lock. "About the work you're doing here, the research opportunities."

"And?"

"I think I'm ready to move forward. But I'd like to see more of the operation first. The behind-the-scenes technical aspects."

James's eyes lit up. "Of course! I'd be happy to give you a complete tour. The observation rooms, the control systems, the data collection protocols." He stood, gesturing toward the door. "We could start with the individual therapy suites."

"Actually," I said, setting my bag down beside his desk, "I was hoping to see how you handle the more challenging scenarios. The ones that require direct intervention."

"Direct intervention?"

"When subjects resist the process. When they try to use safe words or break character." I met his eyes steadily. "I assume not everyone cooperates with your research."

James's expression shifted, becoming more calculating. "That's . . . a sensitive area of our methodology. We have very specific protocols for handling resistance."

"I'm sure you do."

Something in my tone made him step back slightly. Good. Let him start to understand that this conversation wasn't going the way he'd expected.

"Britney, I'm not sure—"

"Show me the restraint systems," I said, reaching into my bag. "Show me how you keep people from leaving when they want to."

James's face went pale as he saw the syringe in my hand. "What are you doing?"

"Research. The kind that reveals fundamental truths about human nature." I smiled, using his own words against him. "You said you wanted to show people what it feels like to be truly helpless, to be at the mercy of someone who enjoys causing pain."

"You're insane."

"I'm justice." I moved around his desk, cutting off his path to the door. "You've been torturing people, James. Breaking them down and calling it therapy. Did you really think no one would ever make you answer for that?"

He lunged for the panic button on his desk, but I was faster. The ketamine went into his neck before he could make a sound, the fast-acting formula I'd gotten from Stu's police contacts taking effect within seconds.

James staggered, his eyes wide with shock and growing confusion. "You can't . . . this is . . ."

"This is what happens when someone finally says enough."

He collapsed into his chair, conscious but unable to move effectively. I'd calculated the dose perfectly—enough to paralyze him but not enough to knock him unconscious. I wanted him awake for what came next.

"Let me tell you what's going to happen, Dr. James Wylder," I said, pulling zip ties from my bag. "You're going to experience your own methodology. You're going to find out what it feels like when someone else has complete control over whether you live or die."

I secured his wrists to the chair arms, then his ankles to the legs. The same kind of restraints he used on his victims, probably purchased from the same medical supply company.

"The beautiful thing about your facility," I continued, checking my work, "is how well you've soundproofed everything. All these rooms designed to contain screaming, to keep the neighbors from hearing what you do to people."

James tried to speak, but the ketamine had affected his vocal cords. Only weak gasps came out.

"Don't worry, the paralysis is temporary. You'll be able to talk soon enough. I want to hear you beg."

I pulled my knife from the bag and held it where he could see it clearly. The blade caught the office lighting, throwing sharp reflections across his terrified face.

"This is for Marcus. Remember Marcus? The twenty-three-year-old with authority figure trauma? You locked him in one of your therapy suites and tortured him for two hours while taking notes on his psychological breakdown."

The knife bit into his forearm, drawing a thin line of blood. James's eyes went wide, his breathing becoming rapid and shallow.

"And this," I said, making another cut on his other arm, "is for Maria and David Santos. The couple you were torturing tonight when I arrived. Did you enjoy watching them beg for mercy while you took notes?"

As the ketamine wore off and James regained the ability to speak, his voice came out as a broken whisper. "Please . . . I was helping them . . . it was therapy . . ."

"It was torture. You were breaking people for your own sick pleasure and convincing yourself it was research."

I made several more shallow cuts, watching him writhe against the restraints. Each slice was deliberate, calculated to cause maximum pain without ending his life too quickly. I wanted him to experience the same helplessness his victims had felt.

"The difference between you and me," I said, positioning the knife over his chest, "is that you tortured innocent people. I only kill monsters."

I looked directly into his eyes, wanting him to see exactly who was ending his miserable life.

"This is for all of them, James. Every person you broke. Every life you destroyed. Every scream you ignored."

The knife went into his heart with one powerful thrust. His eyes went wide with shock, then pain, then nothing.

Dr. James Wylder was finally, permanently quiet.

I spent the next twenty minutes cleaning up. Blood from the cuts I'd made, fingerprints from surfaces I'd touched, any trace that I'd been here. Then I wrapped his body in the plastic sheeting I'd brought, systematic and thorough.

My phone buzzed: *Outside. All clear?*

Give me five minutes. Back entrance.

Stu was waiting by the rear exit when I opened the door, dressed in dark clothes and carrying a large duffel bag. He took one look at the wrapped body and nodded.

"Clean?"

"Spotless. His office looks exactly like it did when I arrived."

Together, we loaded James into the duffel bag and carried him out to Stu's car. The parking lot was empty except for James's BMW, sitting exactly where he'd left it.

"Marina?" I asked.

"Boat's prepped and fueled. We'll be back home by midnight."

As we drove to the marina in separate cars, I felt that familiar sense of completion settling over me. James Wylder was dead. His facility would be shut down. His victims could finally have peace.

And I could go back to being just Britney Cage, small business owner from Tampa.

At least until the next monster needed killing.

Twenty-Three

I SLEPT BETTER SUNDAY night than I had in weeks.

For the first time since I'd discovered Nightmares Unleashed, I didn't wake up thinking about murder. No calculating James's routine, no planning his death, no rage building in my chest every time I thought about his victims.

James Wylder was gone. Permanently.

I made coffee and fed Minion, who seemed to sense my improved mood. She actually purred while eating instead of inhaling her food and disappearing. Even my cat knew the difference.

Stu emerged from the bedroom around eight, looking more rested than he had in days.

"Sleep well?" he asked, settling into the chair across from me with his own coffee.

"Like the dead. You?"

"Best I've slept in months." He studied my face. "You look different."

"Different how?"

"Peaceful. Like you're not carrying the weight of the world anymore."

He was right. The constant tension in my shoulders was gone. The tight feeling in my chest had disappeared. For the first time in weeks, I felt like I could breathe properly.

"Think anyone's found him missing yet?" I asked.

"Probably not until tomorrow morning. Monday's when people start asking questions about weekend disappearances."

We spent Sunday in blissful normalcy. Coffee on the back patio, a lazy trip to the farmers market, reorganizing the spare bedroom we'd been putting off for months. For once, domestic life felt genuine rather than performed.

But Monday morning brought the real test.

I was in the office early, handling client calls and trying to focus on legitimate business when my phone rang. Unknown number.

"Passing Through, Britney speaking."

"Ms. Cage? This is Detective Rodriguez with Tampa PD. I was hoping I could ask you a few questions about Dr. James Wylder."

My heart rate spiked, but I kept my voice calm. "James? What about him?"

"He's been reported missing. His colleagues say he didn't show up for work today, and he had a faculty meeting Friday that he missed without explanation. We're trying to track his movements over the weekend."

"I see. How can I help?"

"We understand you've been attending some of his presentations and working with him on a potential business partnership. When did you last speak with him?"

I took a breath, running through the timeline. "Thursday, I think. I stopped by his facility to discuss Saturday's observation session."

"Saturday's session?"

"He invited me to observe a couples therapy session at his research facility. Something called Nightmares Unleashed."

"And did you attend this session?"

"Yes, I was there Saturday evening. Around eight o'clock."

"How long did you stay?"

"Not long. Maybe an hour? I left before the session was finished—it was pretty intense, and I wasn't feeling well."

"Did Dr. Wylder seem normal to you? Anything unusual about his behavior?"

"He seemed excited about the research, like always. Very focused on his work."

"And that was the last time you saw him?"

"Yes. We were supposed to meet again this week to discuss the business aspects, but we hadn't scheduled anything specific yet."

Detective Rodriguez asked a few more questions about the facility, the other staff I'd seen, whether James had mentioned any threats or personal problems. I answered everything honestly - or as honestly as possible.

"Thank you for your time, Ms. Cage. If you think of anything else that might be helpful, please give me a call."

After I hung up, I sat back in my chair and processed what I'd learned. James was officially missing as of Monday morning. The police were asking routine questions, tracking his movements. Nothing unusual yet.

I called Stu and left a voicemail about the detective's call, then tried to focus on work. But my mind kept running through the conversation, analyzing every word for potential problems.

By lunch, I'd convinced myself the call was exactly what it seemed - routine questioning of someone who'd been in contact with a missing person. Nothing more.

Around two, Julie called.

"You sound different today," she said after we'd exchanged greetings.

"Different how?"

"I don't know. Lighter? Like you've solved some big problem that was bothering you."

You're not wrong.

"Just feeling good. Sometimes things work out the way they're supposed to."

"Work stuff?"

"Something like that." I leaned back in my chair, genuinely relaxed for the first time in weeks.

"Well, whatever it is, I'm glad. Listen, I was calling to see if you and Stu want to come over for dinner tomorrow night. Nothing fancy - just grilling burgers and hanging out. Brian's been asking when Uncle Stu's coming back over."

"That sounds perfect. What time? And what, no Aunt Brit? I'm wounded."

Julie laughed. "Oh please, you know Brian adores you too. But Stu lets him get away with more."

"Fair point."

"Six-thirty?"

"Perfect. See you then."

We chatted for a few more minutes about everyday things - Brian's latest school project, Cody's promotion, the vacation she was planning for next month. The kind of conversation we'd been missing while I was so consumed with hunting James.

When I hung up, I realized I hadn't thought about murder or James or police investigations once during our entire call. For twenty minutes, I'd just been Britney Cage.

It felt good.

But that evening, alone in my office after Barb had gone home, something unexpected happened. For the first time since I'd started hunting James, I sat in complete silence and really processed what I'd done.

I'd killed him. With my own hands. Felt his pulse stop under my fingers.

The memory should have brought satisfaction, and it did. But underneath that satisfaction was something else - a strange emptiness where the rage had been. For weeks, fury had driven every decision, every breath. Now that the source was gone, I felt almost. . . hollow.

I pushed the feeling away and focused on reviewing contracts until Stu got home.

Tuesday brought a different kind of test, and a different kind of reckoning.

I woke before dawn from a dream that wasn't quite a nightmare. In it, James had been sitting across from me at Bern's, explaining his expansion plans. But instead of feeling disgusted, dream-Britney had been fascinated. Intrigued by the psychological manipulation, the control, the power over other people's minds.

I sat up in bed, disturbed not by the dream itself, but by how right it had felt. How easily I could have been drawn into his world if I hadn't seen what he did to his victims.

That's not who you are, I told myself. *You're already a monster, but you're a monster with rules. You aren't like the rest of them.*

But the line felt thinner than it used to.

Stu stirred beside me. "You okay?"

"Just a weird dream. Go back to sleep."

I got up and made coffee, sitting on the back patio as the sun rose. Minion appeared and settled on my lap, purring as I scratched behind her ears. Normal morning routine, but everything felt slightly off-kilter.

My phone buzzed with a text from Julie: *Still on for dinner tonight?*

Dinner. Right. Normal social obligations that required me to act like someone who hadn't committed murder three days ago.

Absolutely. See you at six-thirty.

I tried to focus on normal work at the office that morning. But I kept catching myself analyzing clients' voices for signs of deception, noting body language that suggested vulnerability or psychological manipulation. Professional skills that had suddenly become more acute after witnessing James's methods.

Around noon, I realized I was doing exactly what James had probably done - using legitimate psychological knowledge for darker purposes. The recognition made my stomach turn.

Stop it, I told myself. *You're not him. You'll never be him.*

But I couldn't shake the feeling that killing James had changed something fundamental in how I saw people. Like I'd absorbed some of his clinical detachment along with his death.

I was at my desk reviewing placement contracts when Barb knocked on my door Tuesday afternoon.

"There's someone here to see you," she said. "Says it's about that psychology research you've been involved with."

My stomach dropped, but I kept my expression neutral. "Send them back."

A woman in her forties walked into my office, dressed professionally but with the kind of observant eyes that screamed law enforcement.

"Ms. Cage? I'm Detective Celia Vasquez with Tampa PD. I was hoping we could talk about Dr. James Wylder."

Different detective. Shit.

"Of course. Please, sit." I gestured to the chair across from my desk. "Though I already spoke with Detective Rodriguez yesterday."

"I know. I'm following up on a few things." She pulled out a notebook. "You mentioned attending a session at Nightmares Unleashed on Saturday night."

"That's right."

"We've been trying to access the facility, but it's been locked down since Sunday. Dr. Wylder's business partner says they haven't heard from him since Friday."

I nodded like this was new information, filing it away for later analysis.

"Tell me about Saturday night," Detective Vasquez said. "Walk me through exactly what happened."

I repeated the same story I'd told Detective Rodriguez, keeping the details consistent. Arrived around eight, observed part of a couples session, left early because I wasn't feeling well.

"Did you see Dr. Wylder after the session ended?"

"No. I left while the couple was still in their session. James was focused on his work - I didn't want to interrupt."

"And you drove straight home?"

"Yes."

"Anyone who can verify that?"

"My fiancé. He was home when I got there."

Detective Vasquez made notes, then looked up at me with those sharp eyes. "What was your impression of the facility? Did anything seem off to you?"

I thought carefully before answering. "It was very professional. High-tech equipment, medical-grade security. More sophisticated than I'd expected."

"And the therapy session you observed - how would you describe it?"

"Intense. The couple seemed distressed by whatever scenarios they were experiencing. That's part of why I left early—it was hard to watch."

"Did Dr. Wylder explain his methods to you?"

"In general terms. He called it exposure therapy, helping people confront their fears in a controlled environment."

Detective Vasquez asked a few more questions about the staff I'd seen, the facility layout, whether James had mentioned any personal problems or threats. I answered everything truthfully, sticking to what I'd actually observed.

"One last question," she said, closing her notebook. "In your professional opinion, did Dr. Wylder seem like someone who might just disappear without warning?"

I considered this carefully. "No. He was very committed to his work, very excited about expanding the program. He seemed like someone with long-term plans."

"Thank you for your time, Ms. Cage. Here's my card if you think of anything else."

After she left, I sat in my office processing the conversation. Two detectives asking questions meant the investigation was more serious than routine missing person inquiries. But they were still fishing, looking for leads rather than following concrete evidence.

The fact that the facility had been locked down since Sunday was interesting. Dr. Martinez - whoever she was - had probably panicked when James didn't show up and called the police immediately.

But if they'd found any evidence of foul play, Detective Vasquez would have asked very different questions. The tone would have been accusatory rather than information-gathering.

I was still in the clear. For now.

But that night, lying in bed beside Stu, I found myself replaying both detective interviews in obsessive detail. Not because I was worried about my answers - they'd been perfect, consistent, believable. But because I'd noticed something disturbing about myself during those conversations.

I'd enjoyed them.

Not just the successful deception, though that was satisfying. I'd enjoyed the psychological chess game, the careful dance of truth and lies, the way I could guide Detective Vasquez's questions in the direction I wanted them to go. There had been a thrill in sitting across from law enforcement, knowing I'd committed murder, and watching them treat me as a helpful witness instead of a suspect.

It reminded me uncomfortably of the excitement I'd seen in James's eyes when he watched his victims suffer.

You're nothing like him, I told myself firmly. *He tortured innocent people. You killed a monster.*

But the comparison wouldn't leave me alone. I got up, careful not to wake Stu, and went downstairs to make tea. Minion followed me, winding around my ankles as I moved through the kitchen.

Standing at the sink, looking out at the dark backyard, I forced myself to confront what was really bothering me. Killing James had been necessary, justified, the right thing to do. But somewhere in the process - maybe during those weeks of watching him, maybe during the kill itself, maybe during these police interviews - I'd started to understand him.

Not sympathize with him. Never that. But understand the psychology behind his actions, the rush of power and control, the intellectual satisfaction of manipulating people who had no idea they were being manipulated.

The thought terrified me more than any detective ever could.

Twenty-Four

WEDNESDAY MORNING BROUGHT THE news I'd been expecting.

The Tampa Bay Times ran a small article on page three: "Local Psychology Professor Missing." It was basic information - James Wylder, adjunct professor at USF, missing since Saturday, police investigating. No mention of Nightmares Unleashed or his research methods.

By Thursday, the story had grown. More details about his work, quotes from colleagues expressing concern, a photo from his faculty profile. Still nothing about the true nature of his operation.

I read every article, watched every news segment, monitoring how the story was being told. The media was painting James as a dedicated researcher and innovative therapist. If they only knew what he'd really been doing to those people.

Thursday afternoon brought an unexpected development. A client called asking if I'd heard about "that psychology professor who's been in the news."

"Dr. Wylder? Yes, I saw the reports. Terrible situation."

"I actually went to one of his presentations last month. He was talking about workplace stress management. Seemed like a nice enough guy, though a little intense."

My blood chilled. "What kind of presentation?"

"Oh, you know, the usual corporate wellness stuff. Managing difficult employees, identifying stress indicators, that sort of thing. My company's been looking into bringing him in for some training sessions."

After I hung up, I sat back in my chair, processing this new information. James hadn't just been running his torture facility - he'd been expanding his reach into the legitimate business world. Just like I'd approached him.

The irony wasn't lost on me. While I'd been pretending to consider a business partnership to get closer to him, he'd been putting me through his psychological torture during that VIP preview. Two predators circling each other - I thought I was hunting him, but he'd been trying to break me down from the moment we met.

But this client's call revealed something bigger. James had been giving corporate presentations, studying potential victims under the guise of professional development.

How many corporate presentations had he given? How many boardrooms had he sat in, cataloguing weaknesses like a predator selecting prey?

The scope of his operation was bigger than I'd realized. And I'd stopped it just in time.

But the thought that bothered me most was how easily he'd infiltrated the legitimate business world. How many other monsters were doing the same thing right now - hiding behind professional facades while hunting their next victims?

I found myself opening my laptop and searching for James's speaking engagements. Within minutes, I'd found references to presentations at three major Tampa companies, two consulting firms, and a law office. All within the past six months.

Workplace stress management. Employee psychological profiling. Conflict resolution.

All legitimate-sounding topics that would give him access to detailed information about employees, their personal struggles, their vulnerabilities. He'd been building a database of potential victims, and the companies had been paying him to do it.

The realization made my stomach turn. How many people had attended those presentations thinking they were getting help with workplace issues, never knowing they were being evaluated as potential torture subjects?

I spent the next hour researching his client list, cross-referencing with missing persons reports and unexplained disappearances. The pattern that emerged was subtle but unmistakable - a slight uptick in missing persons cases in areas where James had given presentations.

Nothing dramatic enough to trigger alarm bells. Just enough to provide him with a steady stream of victims who wouldn't be immediately missed or connected to him.

Friday brought Detective Rodriguez back to my office.

"We found Dr. Wylder's car," he said without preamble.

My heart rate spiked, but I kept my expression neutral. "Where?"

"Airport long-term parking. Looks like it's been there since sometime Saturday night or early Sunday morning."

Shit. How did I miss that?

"That's. . . unexpected," I said. "When we spoke Saturday, he didn't mention any travel plans."

"Did he seem like the type to take off without warning? Maybe he was under more stress than he let on?"

I shook my head. "He seemed excited about his work, very engaged. But I didn't know him personally - we only had a professional relationship."

"His credit cards haven't been used since Saturday afternoon. No airline tickets, no hotel reservations, no cell phone activity."

"That doesn't sound good."

"No, it doesn't." Detective Rodriguez studied my face. "Ms. Cage, I have to ask - is there anything about Saturday night that you didn't mention before? Anything that seemed unusual, even if it didn't seem important at the time?"

I thought carefully, running through the timeline. "Actually, now that you mention it, James did seem more excited than usual. Almost manic. But I assumed it was because he was passionate about his research."

"Manic how?"

"Talking faster, more animated than I'd seen him before. Like he was anticipating something big."

Detective Rodriguez made notes. "Anything else?"

"There was another car in the parking lot when I arrived. I assumed it belonged to staff or the couple participating in the session."

"Can you describe it?"

"Dark sedan, I think. I didn't pay much attention—I was focused on getting inside."

All of this was true. There had been other cars, James had seemed excited, and his behavior could easily be interpreted as manic in retrospect.

"Thank you. This helps us understand his state of mind."

After he left, I realized the investigation was shifting. Finding James's car at the airport suggested he'd left voluntarily, which was exactly what I'd hoped they'd conclude.

The afternoon brought another unexpected visitor - not a detective this time, but a woman in an expensive suit who introduced herself as Dr. Jennifer Martinez.

"I'm Dr. Wylder's business partner," she said, settling into the chair across from my desk. "I understand you were working with him on some consulting opportunities."

This was the mysterious Dr. Martinez the police had mentioned. Up close, she looked tired and stressed, like someone whose world had just imploded.

"That's right. Though we were still in the preliminary stages."

"The police said you attended a session at our facility Saturday night."

"Yes. James invited me to observe a couples therapy session."

Dr. Martinez studied my face carefully. "What was your impression?"

An interesting question. Not "how was it?" or "what did you think?" but specifically my impression. Like she was trying to gauge how much I'd really understood about what I'd witnessed.

"Intense," I said. "Cutting-edge technology, very sophisticated approach. Though I have to admit, some of the methods seemed quite aggressive."

"James was passionate about pushing boundaries. Sometimes too passionate." She paused. "I don't suppose he mentioned any travel plans to you?"

"No. We were supposed to meet this week to discuss business aspects."

"I see." Dr. Martinez opened her purse and pulled out a business card. "If you hear from him, would you please call me immediately? I'm. . . concerned about his state of mind."

After she left, I found myself wondering how much Dr. Martinez really knew about James's operation. Was she a willing participant, or had she been kept in the dark about the true nature of his "research"?

The way she'd asked about my "impression" of the session suggested she knew it was more than standard therapy. But her obvious stress and the fact that she'd dissolved the business so quickly could mean she'd been as much a victim as anyone else.

I made a mental note to keep tabs on her. If she'd been complicit, she might try to restart the operation elsewhere. If she'd been innocent, she might need protection from James's other associates - assuming he'd had any.

Either way, her visit confirmed that the business was effectively dead. Without James, there was no Nightmares Unleashed. His victims were safe, at least from that particular monster.

But as I sat alone in my office after she left, I couldn't shake the feeling that I was missing something. Some piece of the puzzle that would explain how James had built such an elaborate operation without attracting more attention.

Money. It always came back to money. Someone had been funding his research, providing the equipment, covering the overhead. James might have been the face of the operation, but he wasn't working alone.

I spent another hour searching for information about Nightmares Unleashed's funding sources. Most of it was buried behind corporate shells and LLC formations, but I managed to trace some connections to a venture capital firm in Orlando and what looked like federal research grants.

Government money. Jesus Christ, taxpayers had been funding his torture operation.

The more I dug, the more complicated the picture became. James hadn't been a lone wolf - he'd been part of a network. And killing him might not have been enough to stop what he'd started.

That evening, Stu and I went to dinner at Julie's as planned. It was exactly what I needed - an evening of normalcy, of being Aunt Brit and enjoying time with people who had no idea what I'd been through.

Brian showed us his latest school project - a diorama of the solar system that he'd built with meticulous attention to detail. Stu helped him adjust the positioning of Mars while I helped Julie in the kitchen.

"You seem more relaxed than you have in weeks," Julie observed as we prepared the salad.

"Work's been stressful lately, but things are settling down."

"Good. You were starting to worry me."

If only she knew what I'd actually been dealing with.

We ate on the back patio, Brian chattering about school and friends and his upcoming birthday party. Normal kid stuff that felt like a balm after everything I'd been processing.

"Uncle Stu," Brian said during dessert, "will you teach me to tie different knots? My scout leader said you know lots of them."

Stu glanced at me, and I saw a flicker of something in his eyes. Knots. Like the ones we'd used on James.

"Sure, buddy. Next time I come over, we'll practice some basic ones."

The conversation moved on, but I caught Stu's eye and gave him a small nod. We were both thinking about Saturday night, about the ropes and restraints, about how those skills had served a very different purpose than Boy Scout camping.

After we got home, I found myself standing in the bathroom, staring at my reflection in the mirror. I looked the same as always - same face, same hair, same eyes. But something fundamental had changed, and I wasn't sure the person looking back at me was someone I recognized anymore.

What are you becoming? I asked my reflection silently.

The woman in the mirror didn't answer, but I could see something new in her eyes. A sharpness that hadn't been there before. A calculating quality that reminded me uncomfortably of the look I'd seen in James's eyes when he studied his victims.

I touched the glass, trying to reconcile the familiar features with this growing sense of alienation from myself. When had I started analyzing everyone around me for weaknesses? When had I begun automatically cataloguing the exact words that would break someone if I needed them to?

Since James, I realized. *Since I watched him work.*

The thought should have disturbed me more than it did. Instead, I found myself fascinated by the transformation. Like a scientist observing an interesting mutation.

I pulled my hair back and leaned closer to the mirror, studying my own micro-expressions. What would James have seen if he'd been analyzing me? What vulnerabilities would he have identified?

Abandonment issues. Need for control. Deep-seated fear of becoming like the monsters you hunt.

The last one hit like a physical blow because it was so obviously true. And because recognizing it meant I was already halfway there.

I stood in that bathroom for nearly twenty minutes, having a silent conversation with my reflection, trying to figure out where the line was between necessary evolution and dangerous corruption.

When I finally turned away from the mirror, I still didn't have an answer. But I had a new understanding of why some people became monsters gradually, one small compromise at a time.

And I had a new fear that I might be walking that same path, one dead body at a time.

Now I just had to wait and see if they bought it.

Twenty-Five

The nightmares started three days after Detective Rodriguez's final call.

Not the usual kind - these were different. Clinical. In them, I was the one behind the desk, taking notes while subjects described their deepest fears. I'd wake up with fragments of psychological profiles floating through my mind, detailed breakdowns of people I'd never met.

But the most disturbing part wasn't the dreams themselves. It was how much I enjoyed them.

By the second week, James Wylder had become yesterday's news. The police investigation had officially shifted to treating his disappearance as voluntary, and the media had moved on to fresher scandals. The Nightmares Unleashed facility remained closed, Dr. Martinez had apparently dissolved the business and left town, probably to avoid questions about their methods.

I'd gone back to my normal routine - running the temp agency, having lunch with Julie, going to dinner at Joe's, girls' nights. The rage and tension that had consumed me for weeks was gone.

But other changes had taken their place.

I'd started noticing things I'd never paid attention to before. The way clients shifted when they lied about their qualifications. Barb's micro-expressions when she was frustrated but trying to hide it. The tells that revealed when Julie was worried about something she didn't want to discuss.

James's psychological training had rubbed off on me, leaving me with unwanted insights into human behavior. I catalogued people's vulnerabilities without meaning to, noted the exact words that would cut deepest if I wanted to hurt them.

The knowledge felt dangerous.

This is how it starts, I thought during a particularly disturbing moment when I caught myself mentally breaking down Julie's psychological defenses while she talked about Brian's problems at school. *This is how monsters are made.*

Recognizing it didn't make it stop. If anything, the awareness made it worse because now I was conscious of every predatory thought, every moment when I analyzed instead of listened.

Julie was worried about Brian getting picked on by older kids. Normal maternal concern that she was sharing with a trusted friend. But all I could think about was how that concern could be weaponized - how someone could use her love for her son to manipulate her.

Stop it, I told myself. *She's your friend, not your target.*

The thoughts kept coming anyway. Automatic and unwelcome. Like a new language I couldn't stop speaking.

A perfect example came during a client meeting on Tuesday morning. A middle-aged man named Robert was interviewing for a management position at one of our corporate clients. Within five minutes, I'd identified his core insecurities: fear of being seen as outdated, desperate need for validation from authority figures, deep shame about his working-class background.

The old me would have focused on his qualifications and personality fit. The new me was calculating how to manipulate him if I needed to.

What the hell is wrong with you? I thought, forcing myself to focus on legitimate interview questions.

The damage was done. I could see Robert's psychological profile as clearly as if James had drawn me a diagram. Every nervous laugh, every defensive posture, every attempt to oversell his credentials - it painted a picture of a man who could be broken with the right pressure.

The realization made me sick to my stomach.

I'd also started sleeping differently. Not better or worse, exactly, but deeper. More dreamless. As if some part of my subconscious had decided that nothing in sleep could be more intense than what I'd experienced while awake.

When I did dream, the dreams were different too. More vivid, more psychological. I'd find myself in scenarios where I was the one conducting experiments, studying subjects, breaking down their defenses with clinical precision.

In one particularly disturbing dream, I'd been sitting across from Brian - sweet, innocent Brian - taking notes as he described his worst fears. Dream-me had been fascinated by his psychological makeup, making plans to exploit his vulnerabilities for some unnamed purpose.

I woke up from that one in a cold sweat, horrified by my subconscious mind's willingness to turn even a child into a potential victim.

This has to stop, I told myself. *This isn't who you are.*

But was that true anymore? Or was this exactly who I was becoming?

Stu had noticed the change. "You used to toss and turn," he mentioned one morning. "Now you sleep like someone who's made peace with something."

He wasn't wrong. Killing James had brought a sense of completion I'd never experienced with my other victims. Maybe because his crimes had been ongoing, immediate, requiring urgent action. Maybe because I'd witnessed them firsthand rather than just learning about them after the fact.

Or maybe because something fundamental had shifted in how I understood the relationship between predator and prey.

The physical changes were subtle but persistent. My appetite had changed - I craved protein more than usual, as if my body was still processing the violence. I found myself flexing my hands throughout the day, remembering the feel of James's throat under my fingers.

Even my relationship with Minion had evolved. She seemed to sense something different about me, spending more time nearby but maintaining a slight distance. Like she recognized a fellow predator but wasn't sure if I was still safe.

Wednesday brought an unexpected reminder of the case when Barb mentioned seeing a news report about missing persons cases in Florida.

"Did you see they're linking that psychology professor to some kind of pattern?" she asked during our morning coffee.

My blood chilled. "What kind of pattern?"

"Something about other missing people who'd been involved with experimental therapy programs. The reporter was saying there might be more victims than they originally thought."

I forced myself to look interested rather than alarmed. "That's terrible. Do they have any leads?"

"Doesn't sound like it. But they're reopening some cold cases, looking for connections."

After Barb left my office, I sat staring at my computer screen, processing this development. If the police were connecting James to other missing persons, it meant his operation had been bigger than I'd realized. How many people had he destroyed before I stopped him?

The thought should have made me feel vindicated. Instead, it made me feel guilty for not acting sooner.

But there was something else, something darker that I didn't want to acknowledge: part of me was impressed by the scope of his operation. The sophistication, the long-term planning, the psychological complexity. James had been a monster, but he'd also been brilliant.

And I'd absorbed some of that brilliance along with his death.

The thought that bothered me most, the one I tried to push away but couldn't quite manage, was simple: I missed the hunt.

Not James specifically. Good riddance to that piece of shit. But I missed the intellectual challenge of studying a target, learning their patterns, finding their weaknesses. I missed the satisfaction of planning a perfect kill, the rush of execution, the sense of righteous purpose that came from removing evil from the world.

My other kills had been spread out over years, with long periods of normal life in between. But the intensity of hunting James - the weeks of constant focus, the psychological complexity of his operation, the elaborate planning required - had been like a drug. And now I was coming down from the high.

Thursday evening, I found myself doing something I'd never done before: actively looking for my next target.

I started with local news websites, scanning for stories about corruption, abuse, exploitation. Then I moved to social media, looking for patterns of behavior that suggested hidden darkness. Finally, I found myself browsing true crime forums, reading about unsolved cases and unpunished criminals.

Research, I told myself. *Just staying informed about the monsters in my community.*

But deep down, I knew I was hunting again.

The process felt different this time. More methodical, more scientific. Instead of reacting to obvious predators who crossed my path, I was actively seeking them out using criteria I'd absorbed from James.

Look for the ones who work with vulnerable populations, my mind whispered. *Teachers, counselors, coaches, clergy. People with built-in access and trust.*

Study their social media for signs of narcissism, manipulation, inappropriate boundary crossing.

Check for gaps in their employment history, unexplained relocations, complaints that were dropped or settled quietly.

Where had these thoughts come from? This wasn't how I'd found my previous targets. This was systematic, professional, predatory.

I wasn't a vigilante. I just killed the bad people. But this felt different - like I was hunting for sport rather than justice.

This was how James would have hunted.

The realization should have stopped me cold. Instead, it energized me. Because if I could think like a monster, I could catch monsters more efficiently than ever before.

But at what cost?

I spent three hours that night building psychological profiles of potential targets, cross-referencing public records and social media posts, looking for patterns that suggested hidden darkness.

By the time I closed my laptop, I had a list of twelve names. Twelve people who might be monsters, might be worthy of my attention, might deserve to die.

The fact that I'd compiled such a list so easily should have terrified me.

Instead, it felt like coming home.

The realization should have worried me. A normal person would be concerned about developing a taste for murder, about crossing lines that couldn't be uncrossed.

But I wasn't normal. I'd known that for years.

The question was whether I was becoming something worse than I'd been before. Something more like the monsters I hunted.

Friday brought the final piece of evidence that James's disappearance was being written off as voluntary. Detective Rodriguez called to let me know they were scaling back the active investigation.

"Without any evidence of foul play, we're treating this as a missing person case rather than a potential homicide," he explained. "Dr. Wylder's financial troubles were more serious than we initially realized. Looks like he had good reason to disappear."

"Financial troubles?"

"Gambling debts, mainly. Significant ones. Plus some irregularities with his research funding that were about to come to light. Running away makes more sense than we thought."

Perfect. James's own vices were providing cover for his murder. The irony was delicious.

"I hope he's okay," I said, injecting just the right amount of concern into my voice.

"So do we. But honestly, this feels like someone who made a calculated decision to start over somewhere else."

After hanging up, I leaned back in my chair and smiled. The case was effectively closed, James's victims were safe, and I'd gotten away with murder once again.

But instead of the satisfaction I usually felt at this point, there was something else: hunger.

Hunger for the next hunt, the next monster, the next opportunity to use what James had taught me about the psychology of predators.

The student had surpassed the teacher, and now she was ready to hunt again.

Twenty-Six

Saturday night, Stu and I sat on the back patio with wine and cheese, watching the sunset over Tampa Bay. The air was warm but not humid, perfect for sitting outside and talking. Or in this case, processing.

"How are you feeling about everything?" he asked. "Really feeling, not just the surface level."

I considered the question seriously. "Different. Changed, I think."

"How so?"

"James wasn't like the others. He was more. . . sophisticated. More psychological. Killing him was necessary, but it was also educational in ways I didn't expect."

Stu nodded, understanding immediately what I meant. "You learned something about yourself."

"Yeah. And I'm not sure I like what I learned."

We sat in silence for a moment, watching a pelican dive for fish in the distance.

"Tell me," he said.

"I understand him now. Not his motivations - those were sick and selfish. But his methods. The way he read people, manipulated them, found their psychological pressure points. I can do that now too, and it scares me."

"Because you think it makes you like him?"

"Because I think I might enjoy it too much. More than I already enjoy killing."

Stu reached over and took my hand. "The difference is what you do with that knowledge. James used it to hurt innocent people for his own gratification. You used it to stop him."

"But what if next time I don't use it to stop someone? What if I use it because I can?"

The question hung between us, heavier than the humid evening air.

"Give me an example," Stu said quietly. "What kind of thoughts are you having?"

I hesitated, not sure I wanted to voice what had been going through my mind. But if I couldn't tell Stu, who could I tell?

"Yesterday, Julie was talking about Brian's problems at school. Normal mom stuff - she's worried about him getting picked on. But while she was talking, all I could think about was how someone could use that worry against her. How her love for Brian makes her vulnerable to manipulation."

Stu nodded, his expression carefully neutral. "That's not necessarily wrong thinking. Recognizing vulnerabilities can help you protect people."

"But that's not what I was thinking about. I was thinking about how *I* could use it. How I could get

Julie to do anything I wanted by threatening Brian's safety or well-being." The words tasted bitter. "What kind of person thinks that way about their best friend?"

"A person who's been exposed to a master manipulator," Stu said firmly. "A person who's absorbed some dangerous knowledge and is struggling to process it."

"Or a person who's becoming a monster."

"Then I'll stop you," Stu said simply. "Just like you'd stop me if I went too far."

I looked at him, surprised by the certainty in his voice.

"You mean that."

"Absolutely. We're partners, Brit. In everything. That includes keeping each other human."

The word 'human' hit me like a physical blow. Because part of me wasn't sure I qualified anymore.

"What if I don't want to be stopped?" I asked, voicing the fear that had been growing in the back of my mind. "What if this becomes who I am, and I like it too much to change?"

Stu was quiet for a long moment, considering. "Then I guess we'll find out how much I really love you."

"Meaning?"

"Meaning I'll do whatever it takes to save you from yourself. Even if you hate me for it."

The conviction in his voice was both comforting and terrifying. He meant it. He would literally fight me to save me from becoming a monster.

"And if you can't save me?"

"Then I'll make sure you don't hurt innocent people."

We both knew what that meant. If I became something irredeemable, if I crossed the line from justified killer to predator, Stu would stop me permanently.

The thought should have upset me. Instead, it was oddly reassuring. At least one of us was still thinking clearly.

"I've been thinking about hunting again," I admitted. "Looking for the next target."

"Already?"

"I know it's too soon. But the need is there, stronger than it's ever been. Like James awakened something in me."

Stu studied my face in the fading light. "What kind of something?"

"Hunger. Not just for justice, but for the hunt itself. The psychological games, the planning, the power over life and death." I paused, struggling to find the right words. "I think I understand now why some people become serial killers. Not the ones who kill for pleasure, but the ones who kill because they can't stop."

"You're not there yet," Stu said carefully. "But you could be."

"Yeah. I could be."

We sat in silence, both processing the implications of what I'd just admitted. I was walking a tightrope between justice and madness, and the fall could destroy everything I cared about.

"So what do we do?" he asked finally.

"We stick to the plan. Hunt monsters, not innocents. Keep each other grounded. And maybe. . ." I hesitated, then plunged ahead. "Maybe we need to establish some rules. Boundaries that we don't cross."

"Like what?"

"No killing just because we can. No targeting people who haven't earned it. No letting the hunt become more important than the justice." I looked at him. "And if one of us starts to lose it, the other has veto power."

Stu nodded slowly. "I can live with that. Though I have to ask - do you think you're already losing it?"

I considered the question honestly. "I don't know. That's what scares me."

"Well, for what it's worth, the fact that you're worried about it is a good sign. Sociopaths don't question their own morality."

"Maybe not. But they're also really good at convincing themselves they're the heroes of their own stories."

Another silence fell between us, this one heavier than before. I was voicing fears that had been building for weeks, admitting to psychological changes that might be irreversible.

"Any regrets?" he asked, changing the subject slightly.

"Do I ever?"

"Good point. He deserved everything he got."

I leaned against Stu's shoulder, feeling content despite the psychological turmoil. This was what I loved about him - he could see my darkness without flinching, could love me despite the monster I was becoming.

"I love you," Stu said suddenly. "Whatever you become, whatever we become together, that won't change."

"Even if I become something monstrous?"

"Especially then. Monsters need love too. Maybe more than anyone else."

I smiled, but it felt different than my usual post-kill satisfaction. More complex. More uncertain. More human, in its imperfection.

"Think we'll do this again?" I asked.

"What, kill another monster together?" Stu didn't even hesitate. "Of course. But maybe next time we'll be more careful about the psychological fallout."

"What do you mean?"

"I mean James got under your skin in a way the others didn't. Changed you. We need to watch for that, make sure we don't lose ourselves to the hunt."

He was right. Killing James had been a victory, but it had also been a warning. There was a thin line between justice and obsession, between righteousness and sadism. I'd walked that line with James, and I wasn't sure I'd stayed on the right side of it.

We made a good team, Stu and I. Professional, efficient, completely in sync when it mattered. But we were also changing, evolving into something neither of us fully understood yet.

The world was full of monsters pretending to be normal people. James Wylder had been one of them, and now he was gone.

But there would be others. There always were.

And when I found them, I'd be ready. The question was whether the person doing the hunting would still be someone I recognized in the mirror.

Or whether that even mattered anymore.

As the last light faded from the sky, I made myself a promise: I would hunt again. But I would hunt smart, hunt carefully, and hunt with purpose.

Because the alternative - losing myself completely to the darkness that James had awakened - was a fate worse than death.

At least for now.

Twenty-Seven

THREE WEEKS HAD PASSED since James Wylder disappeared. Three weeks of police interviews, news reports, and the slow fade of public interest. Three weeks of going back to my normal routine while something fundamental had shifted inside me.

I was sitting in my office reviewing contracts when Barb knocked on my door.

"Brit? There's someone here to see you. Says she has a business proposition."

I looked up from the paperwork. "Do we have an appointment scheduled?"

"No, but she says she's with Synergy Publishing. Something about staffing needs."

Synergy Publishing. The name rang a bell, though I couldn't place it immediately. "Send her in."

The woman who walked into my office was exactly what I'd expect from a publishing company - professionally dressed, confident stride, expensive handbag. But there was something else. An intensity in her eyes that reminded me of myself.

"Ms. Cage? I'm Erika Logan, CEO of Synergy Publishing." She extended a manicured hand. "Thank you for seeing me without an appointment."

Erika Logan. Now I remembered where I'd heard that name. Marsha's girlfriend Melissa had mentioned her about a year ago, back at Joe's dinner party. The ruthless publisher taking Tampa by storm.

"Of course. Please, have a seat. What can I do for you?"

Erika settled into the chair across from my desk, crossing her legs. "I'll be direct. My company is expanding rapidly, and we need reliable staffing support. Temporary assistants, copy editors, administrative staff. I've heard excellent things about your agency."

I leaned back in my chair, studying her. Something felt off about this interaction, though I couldn't pinpoint what. "That's flattering. What kind of volume are we talking about?"

"Significant. We're looking at twenty to thirty placements initially, with potential for much more if things go well." She pulled out a folder and slid it across my desk. "I've prepared a preliminary overview of our needs."

I flipped through the documents. Everything looked legitimate - job descriptions, salary ranges, company information. But the way Erika was watching me suggested this wasn't just about staffing.

"This looks comprehensive," I said. "When would you need to start placements?"

"Immediately. We're launching several new imprints next quarter, and we're behind on hiring." She paused, tilting her head slightly. "You know, you look familiar. Have we met before?"

Interesting question. "I don't think so. I'd remember."

"Hmm. Maybe it's just one of those faces." But her expression suggested she wasn't buying her own explanation. "So, are you interested in working together?"

There was something predatory in the way she asked the question. Like this was a test, or a game I wasn't aware I was playing.

"I'm always interested in new business," I said carefully. "Though I do have some questions about your company culture, working conditions, that sort of thing. I like to make sure my temps are going into good environments."

Erika's smile sharpened. "How thorough of you. Most agencies just care about the billable hours."

"I'm not most agencies."

"No, I can see that." She leaned forward slightly. "What if I told you I could offer your people something most companies can't?"

"Such as?"

"Growth opportunities. Real advancement. The chance to discover what they're truly capable of when pushed to their limits."

The way she said it made my skin crawl. There was an undertone that reminded me uncomfortably of James Wylder's sales pitch about "unlocking human potential."

"That sounds. . . intense," I said.

"The best opportunities always are. Some people thrive under pressure. Others. . . well, they reveal their true nature when the facade drops."

There it is. The mask slipping just enough to show me what was underneath. Erika Logan wasn't just a publishing CEO. She was something else entirely.

"I think I need some time to review your proposal," I said, closing the folder.

"Of course. But don't take too long. Opportunities like this don't wait forever." She stood, smoothing her skirt. "I have a feeling we could accomplish great things together, Ms. Cage."

After she left, I sat staring at the folder for a long time. Everything about that interaction had felt like a psychological evaluation. Like she'd been probing for something specific.

I opened my laptop and started researching Synergy Publishing. What I found was. . . interesting.

On the surface, they were exactly what Erika had presented - a growing publishing house with several successful imprints. But when I dug deeper, I found patterns that made my skin crawl.

Authors who'd signed with them and then disappeared from the literary scene entirely. Manuscripts that dealt with psychological trauma, manipulation, control. A company culture described by former employees as "intense" and "psychologically demanding."

And then I found the connection that made everything click.

Dr. James Wylder had been listed as a published author with several Synergy publications - books about overcoming trauma through "exposure therapy" and "controlled psychological intervention."

Erika Logan hadn't come to me for staffing.

She'd come because she knew what had happened to James. And she wanted to see what kind of person I really was.

The question was: what did she plan to do with that information?

Twenty-Eight

THAT NIGHT, I TOLD Stu about Erika's visit.

"So she's connected to James," he said, pouring himself a beer. "That's not good."

"It gets worse. I actually met her about a year ago at Joe's dinner party. Marsha's girlfriend Melissa introduced us - mentioned how Erika was this ruthless publisher taking publishing by storm. I barely paid attention at the time, but now. . ."

"Now she's specifically targeting you."

"Exactly. And I've been reading about her company all afternoon. This woman isn't just running a publishing house - she's building some kind of psychological manipulation empire."

I showed him what I'd found: the pattern of authors disappearing, the focus on trauma-based content, the consulting relationship with James.

"Look at this," I said, pulling up a forum post from a former Synergy employee. "They had mandatory 'team building exercises' that sound like psychological torture. One person claims they had to undergo simulated kidnapping scenarios as part of their job training."

Stu read over my shoulder. "Jesus. So what's her angle with you?"

"I think she knows I killed James. Or at least suspects it."

"How would she know that?"

I thought about the way Erika had watched me during our conversation, the probing questions disguised as small talk.

"Maybe James told her about me before he died. Or maybe she's been tracking the investigation and noticed I was one of the last people to see him alive."

"Or maybe she's just fishing, seeing if she can find out what happened to her consultant."

"Either way, she's dangerous. And she's clearly been planning this approach for a while."

Stu was quiet for a moment, processing this. "So what do we do?"

The answer came to me with startling clarity.

"We do what we always do when we find a monster."

"You want to kill her."

It wasn't a question. Stu knew me well enough to recognize the decision in my voice.

"She's building exactly what James was building, but bigger. More sophisticated. She's turning psychological torture into a business model, and she's expanding."

"So we stop her."

"We stop her."

But even as I said it, I knew this would be different from James. More complicated. Erika wasn't operating from some isolated facility - she had a legitimate business, employees, visibility in the community. Her disappearance would raise questions.

Which meant I'd have to be even more careful. More creative.

The thought should have intimidated me. Instead, I felt that familiar tingle of anticipation.

Erika Logan thought she was hunting me.

In time, she would learn how wrong she was.

Twenty-Nine

Life settled back into its normal rhythm over the next few weeks. Work was busy, the weather was finally cooling down from the brutal summer heat, and I was back to focusing on what mattered: running my business and enjoying the people in my life.

Thursday brought girls' night at The Pub, our usual spot. Julie looked more relaxed than she had in months, actually laughing at Sarah's stories about her latest dating disasters instead of just politely smiling. Even Danielle had made it out, which was a relief since she'd missed the past couple of girls' nights.

"How are you feeling?" I asked her as we settled into our booth.

"Better some days than others," she said with a tired smile. "The doctors are still running tests to figure out what's going on. But I wasn't about to miss hearing about Sarah's latest romantic catastrophe."

"Hey!" Sarah protested, but she was grinning. "My dating life provides valuable entertainment for this group."

"Speaking of which," Julie said, "tell them about the tuxedo t-shirt guy."

"So he shows up to the date wearing a tuxedo t-shirt," Sarah was saying, gesturing wildly with her wine glass. "And when I asked about it, he said he wanted to be 'formal but fun.' I mean, what does that even mean?"

"It means he shops at Spencer's," I said, which sent Julie into a fit of giggles.

"You're terrible," she said, but she was grinning. "Though you're probably not wrong."

It was good to see her like this. The stress of the past few months - Brian's issues at school, work pressure, single mom guilt - had been weighing on her. But tonight she seemed lighter, more like herself.

"How's Brian doing?" I asked when Sarah went to the bathroom.

"Much better. His grades are up, and he's made a few friends in that book club you suggested. He keeps asking when you're coming over for dinner again."

"How about this weekend? I could bring Stu, make it a proper dinner party."

Julie's face lit up. "He'd love that. Fair warning though - he's been reading some fantasy series about dragons, so be prepared for a very detailed plot summary."

"I live for Brian's book reports. They're better than most movies."

When Sarah came back, she launched into another dating horror story, this one involving a guy who'd brought his mother to dinner. By the time we left The Pub, my cheeks hurt from laughing.

Driving home, I felt that familiar sense of contentment that came from spending time with people who knew me - or at least, knew the version of me I chose to show them. It was a good life I'd built here, full of genuine relationships and simple pleasures.

James Wylder was gone, and the world was a better place for it. That was enough.

For now.

Thirty

Saturday afternoon found me in Julie and Cody's kitchen, helping Julie prep for dinner while Brian regaled us with detailed analysis of his latest fantasy novel. Stu and Cody were in the living room, pretending to watch football but actually listening to Brian's enthusiastic plot summary with genuine interest.

"And then the dragon bonds with the farm boy, but it's not just any dragon - it's the last of the ancient fire drakes, and they can only bond with someone who has pure intentions," Brian was explaining as he set the table. "But the evil sorcerer doesn't know this, so when he tries to control the dragon. . ."

"Let me guess," I said, stirring the sauce Julie had handed me. "The dragon incinerates him?"

"No! That's what makes it so good. The dragon refuses to fight at all, which drives the sorcerer crazy because he can't understand why his magic isn't working."

Julie rolled her eyes fondly. "He's been going on like this for three days. Cody and I know this book better than he does at this point."

"It's called world-building, Mom. You have to understand the magic system for the story to make sense."

Stu and Cody wandered into the kitchen together. "Did someone say magic system?" Stu asked. "Because Brian was just explaining to me why fireballs are actually the least efficient combat spell."

"Finally, someone who gets it!" Brian said, launching into another explanation.

Cody caught my eye and we both started laughing. "This is what dinner conversation has been like all week," he said. "I'm starting to dream about dragons."

I caught Julie's eye and we both smiled. This was exactly what I'd needed - normal family chaos, the kind of evening where the biggest drama was whether we'd have enough garlic bread.

Dinner was perfect in its ordinariness. Brian dominated the conversation with book recommendations for all of us, Julie shared funny stories from work, Cody told us about the latest chaos at his architecture firm, and Stu told carefully edited tales from his patrol duties. The wine flowed freely - we'd gone through almost three bottles by the time we reached dessert, leaving all four adults feeling relaxed and happy.

When Brian asked if Stu had ever arrested a real criminal, I watched Stu navigate the question with the skill of someone who knew how to talk to kids.

"Mostly just people having bad days," he said. "Sometimes folks make poor choices when they're upset or scared."

"But what about the really bad guys? Like murderers and stuff?"

Julie shot me an apologetic look, but I just shrugged. Kids were curious about these things.

"That's more detective work," Stu said. "Different department. My job is usually helping people with everyday problems."

After dinner, while Julie, Cody and I cleaned up, Stu and Brian got into a heated discussion about whether magic systems should have clearly defined rules or be more mysterious. I listened to them debate the merits of hard versus soft magic while scraping plates, and felt that familiar warmth that came from being around people who genuinely enjoyed each other's company.

"Thank you for this," Julie said quietly as we loaded the dishwasher. "Brian's been so much happier lately, and I think having you and Stu around helps. He needs more adults in his life who take his interests seriously."

"Plus it gives Cody and me a break from the constant fantasy discussions," Cody added with a grin. "I love the kid, but I can only hear so much about dragon bonding rituals before my brain shuts down."

"Are you kidding? I love listening to him. He's got better taste in books than half my clients."

"Still. It means a lot."

Driving home later, Stu and I were quiet for a while, both of us full and content.

"Good kid," he said finally.

"The best. Julie's done an amazing job with him."

"Reminds me a little of myself at that age. Always reading, always asking questions about how things worked."

I glanced over at him. "Is that when you decided to become a cop?"

"Nah, that came later. Back then I wanted to be a scientist. Thought I'd figure out how everything worked and then fix all the problems."

"What changed your mind?"

Stu was quiet for a moment. "Realized some problems can't be fixed with theory. Sometimes you have to get your hands dirty."

I understood what he meant. Some problems required action, not analysis.

But tonight wasn't about problems or solutions. Tonight was about the simple pleasure of good food, good friends, and the kind of normal life I'd built for myself in Tampa.

It was enough.

Thirty-One

Monday morning started with good news. The Henderson Group called to confirm they wanted to extend their contract with the regulatory compliance specialist I'd placed there.

"She's exactly what we needed," the hiring manager told me. "Professional, knowledgeable, and she's already caught two potential issues that could have cost us significant fines."

"That's wonderful to hear. I'll let her know how pleased you are."

"Actually, we're hoping you might have someone else with similar qualifications. We're expanding the compliance department."

I made notes while we talked, already mentally going through my database of potential candidates. It was the kind of problem I loved having - clients so happy they wanted more of the same.

Barb knocked on my office door as I was hanging up. "Good news?"

"The best kind. Happy client, potential new placement."

"You've been getting a lot of those lately."

She was right. The past few months had been consistently good, with more successful placements than usual and fewer headaches. Maybe I was finally hitting my stride with this business.

Tuesday brought a different kind of challenge. One of my long-term temps, a woman I'd placed at a downtown law firm six months ago, called in tears.

"I don't know what to do," she said. "One of the partners has been making comments, touching my shoulder when he talks to me. It's not anything I can prove, but it makes me uncomfortable."

This was the part of the job I hated - when good people got caught in bad situations. "Have you documented any of it? Dates, times, what was said?"

"Some of it. But I'm scared if I report it, they'll just find a reason to let me go."

"That would be retaliation, which is illegal. But I understand your concern."

We talked through her options. File a complaint with HR, document everything going forward, or I could quietly start looking for a new placement for her. She chose to think about it over the weekend.

After I hung up, I sat staring out my office window, thinking about how many women dealt with this kind of crap at work. It made me angry in a way that felt familiar, like an old friend I'd been trying to avoid.

Wednesday was better. Julie called around lunch to check in.

"How's your week going?" she asked.

"Really good, actually. Had some great client feedback this morning. How about you? How are things at the other office?"

"Busy but good. I placed three people this week, including that accountant we've been trying to match with the right firm for months."

"The one with the nonprofit experience?"

"That's the one. Turns out the small firm in Westchase was exactly what she was looking for. Sometimes patience pays off."

We talked for another twenty minutes about placements, difficult clients, and weekend plans. It was exactly the kind of mid-week check-in that made the difference between a good friendship and a great working relationship.

Thursday afternoon, Stu called while I was reviewing applications for the Henderson Group's new position.

"How's your day going?" he asked.

"Productive. Yours?"

"Quiet, which is good. Had a fender-bender this morning and a noise complaint this afternoon, but nothing too exciting."

"Sometimes boring is better."

"Definitely. Oh, and I heard back about that detective position I applied for. They want to interview me next week."

"Stu, that's fantastic! When?"

"Tuesday afternoon. I'm nervous but excited."

I loved how ambitious he was, always looking for ways to grow and challenge himself. "You're going to do great. They'd be lucky to have you."

"Thanks. I hope they see it that way."

"Nice work, Detective Jones."

"I like the sound of that," he said, and I could hear the smile in his voice.

Friday morning brought an unexpected visit from one of my clients - the owner of a small accounting firm who'd been using my services for almost two years.

"I wanted to stop by in person," she said, settling into the chair across from my desk. "The temp you placed with us last month? We want to offer her a permanent position."

"That's wonderful. She's very talented."

"More than that - she's efficient, detail-oriented, and she gets along well with everyone. Exactly what we needed."

After she left, I called the temp with the good news. Her excitement was infectious, and I found myself smiling as I hung up the phone. These were the moments that made the job worthwhile - when everything aligned and everyone ended up happy.

Stu and I went to our favorite Thai place for dinner Friday night. Over pad thai and spring rolls, we talked about our weeks and made plans for the weekend.

"Want to do something Sunday?" he asked. "I don't have to work, so we could take a day trip somewhere."

"Actually, that sounds perfect. It's been a while since we've done anything spontaneous."

"Beach? Or maybe drive up to Crystal River, see the manatees?"

"Manatees sound amazing. I haven't been there in years."

Saturday was one of those lazy days that felt earned after a busy week. We slept in, had a long breakfast, and spent the afternoon running errands that had been piling up. I decided to make my grandmother's chocolate cake recipe - the one that never failed to impress - just because I felt like baking.

Stu helped, which mostly involved him eating way too much batter and making me laugh.

"You're going to make yourself sick," I warned as he scraped the bowl clean.

"Worth it. This is incredible."

"Save some enthusiasm for the actual cake."

"There's always more enthusiasm where that came from."

Sunday morning dawned bright and clear, perfect weather for a drive to Crystal River. We packed a cooler with drinks and snacks, grabbed our sunglasses, and headed north on Highway 19.

The drive took us through small Florida towns and past sprawling horse farms. With the windows down and music playing, it felt like the kind of road trip we used to take when we were first dating - no agenda, no schedule, just time together.

The manatee tour was everything I'd hoped for. We saw dozens of the gentle giants swimming in the warm springs, some with babies following close behind. There's something peaceful about watching creatures that move through life at their own pace, unbothered by the chaos of the world around them.

"They're so calm," I said as we watched a mother manatee nursing her calf.

"Must be nice, having that kind of serenity."

"Think we'll ever get there?"

Stu considered the question. "Maybe. In our own way."

We drove home as the sun was setting, both of us relaxed and content. It had been exactly the kind of day I needed - no agenda, no stress, just time with the person I loved most.

Monday morning brought me back to reality, but in the best possible way. I was barely through my first cup of coffee when my phone rang.

"Hey, kid. How was your weekend?"

"Joe! Really good, actually. Stu and I went to see the manatees up in Crystal River yesterday."

"That sounds wonderful. Those gentle giants always put things in perspective, don't they?"

"They really do. How are you and Marsha?"

"We're great. Actually, that's why I'm calling. Marsha and I were wondering if you and Stu wanted to come over for dinner this weekend. Maybe Sunday? I know it's been too long since we've all gotten together."

I felt a warm flutter of anticipation. Joe and Marsha's dinners were always something to look forward to - good food, easy conversation, and the kind of family atmosphere I'd never had growing up.

"That sounds perfect. What can we bring?"

"Just yourselves. Oh, and if you happen to have any of that chocolate cake lying around. . ." Joe chuckled. "Marsha's still talking about the one you brought last time."

"I actually just made one yesterday. Perfect timing."

"Excellent. How about six o'clock Sunday?"

"We'll be there. Can't wait."

"Me too, kid. See you then."

After I hung up, I realized I was smiling. Sunday dinner at Joe and Marsha's felt like the perfect way to end what was shaping up to be a really good week.

Thirty-Two

WORK HAD BEEN UNUSUALLY busy lately, which I didn't mind. Three new contracts in two weeks, including a law firm that needed specialized administrative support. Julie was handling most of the placements now, freeing me up to focus on business development and the more complex client relationships.

"The Henderson Group wants to extend Sarah's contract through the end of the year," Julie told me during our Wednesday check-in. "And they're asking if we have anyone else with her skill set."

"That's great news. What about the Morrison account?"

"Still working on that one. They want someone with both legal experience and technical writing skills, which is a pretty specific combination."

I made a note to call a few of my former temps who might be a good fit. One of the things I'd learned over the years was that the best placements often came from people who'd worked with me before and trusted my judgment.

"Oh, and Brian called," Julie added with a grin. "He wants to know if you're free for coffee this weekend. Apparently, he has some urgent book recommendations."

"Of course he does. Tell him Saturday afternoon works."

After Julie left, I spent some time updating client files and reviewing financials. The business was in good shape - better than it had been in years, actually. We'd found our niche in the Tampa market, built a reputation for quality placements, and developed relationships with clients who came back to us again and again.

It was satisfying work, even if it wasn't particularly exciting. There was something to be said for building something useful, something that helped people find jobs and helped businesses find good employees.

My phone rang, pulling me out of my thoughts.

"Passing Through, Britney speaking."

"Ms. Cage? This is Detective Martinez with Tampa PD. I was hoping I could ask you a few follow-up questions about Dr. James Wylder."

My heart rate spiked, but I kept my voice steady. "Of course. Has there been a development in the case?"

"We're closing the file. Dr. Wylder has been officially classified as a voluntary missing person. But I wanted to follow up on a few details before we finalize everything."

"I see. How can I help?"

The questions were routine - confirming the timeline of my interactions with James, clarifying details about the presentation I'd attended. Nothing that suggested they suspected foul play or had any leads pointing in my direction.

"Thank you for your time, Ms. Cage. And if Dr. Wylder should contact you for any reason, please let us know immediately."

"Of course."

After I hung up, I sat back in my chair and processed the conversation. The case was officially closed. James Wylder was presumed to have disappeared voluntarily, probably to start a new life somewhere else. The police had no evidence of foul play, no suspects, no leads.

It was over.

I should have felt relieved, but instead I found myself thinking about the victims James had tortured in his facility. The ones I'd been able to save, and the ones I hadn't. The research data that had been destroyed, ensuring no one else could continue his work.

Justice had been served, even if the official record would never reflect it.

That evening, I made dinner for Stu and me - nothing fancy, just pasta and salad - and told him about the call from Detective Martinez.

"So it's really over," he said.

"Looks like it."

"How do you feel about that?"

I considered the question. "Good, I think. Like we accomplished what we set out to do."

"No regrets?"

"About James? None. He deserved what he got." I twirled pasta around my fork. "I just hope his victims can find some peace, knowing he's gone."

Stu reached across the table and squeezed my hand. "They can, because of what you did."

We finished dinner in comfortable silence, both of us lost in our own thoughts. Outside, the Tampa evening was warm and humid, the kind of weather that made you want to sit on the porch with a cold drink and watch the world go by.

"Want to take a walk?" Stu suggested.

"Sure."

We walked through our neighborhood, past houses where families were settling in for the evening. Children playing in yards, couples walking dogs, the ordinary rhythm of suburban life. It was peaceful in a way that felt earned.

Whatever else happened, we'd made the world a little bit safer. And for now, that was enough.

Thirty-Three

Saturday afternoon, I met Brian for coffee at a new café near his school. He'd discovered the place recently and was excited to show it off, especially their hot chocolate, which he insisted was "actually good" as opposed to the "fake good hot chocolate" served everywhere else.

"The difference is they use real cocoa powder," he explained seriously as we settled into our usual corner table. "Most places just use syrup, which doesn't have the same depth of flavor."

I hid my smile behind my coffee cup. At thirteen, Brian had developed strong opinions about everything from beverage preparation to fantasy world-building, and he expressed them with the kind of confidence I envied.

"So what's the book recommendation this week?" I asked.

His face lit up. "Okay, so you know how I was reading that dragon series? Well, I finished it, and the ending was perfect, but now I need something completely different to cleanse my palate."

"Your palate?"

"Yeah, you know how after you eat something really spicy you need milk? It's the same with books. After epic fantasy, I need something grounded and realistic."

He pulled a paperback from his backpack. "So I'm reading this mystery series about a detective who solves cold cases. It's really good because the author doesn't rely on coincidences - everything the detective figures out, you could figure out too if you were paying attention."

I took the book and read the back cover. It did sound interesting, though I wasn't sure I was in the mood for anything involving murder investigations.

"What made you pick mystery novels?"

Brian shrugged. "I like puzzles. And I like stories where justice actually happens, you know? In real life, bad people get away with stuff all the time. But in a good mystery, the bad guy always gets caught."

There was something in his tone that made me look at him more carefully. "Is everything okay at school?"

"Yeah, mostly. There's this kid who's been picking on some of the younger students, but the teachers never catch him doing it. He's smart about only doing stuff when adults aren't looking."

"That's frustrating."

"It is. But I figure if I can't stop him directly, at least I can make sure the kids he's targeting have someone to sit with at lunch. Sometimes just not being alone is enough."

I felt a surge of pride. Brian was turning into exactly the kind of person the world needed more of - someone who noticed when others were hurting and tried to help.

"That's really thoughtful of you."

"Mom always says that if you see something wrong and you can do something about it, you should. Even if it's just a little thing."

Smart woman, Julie.

We spent the rest of our coffee date talking about books, school, and Brian's plans for high school next year. He was excited about the advanced placement classes but worried about fitting in with older kids.

"The thing is," he said, stirring the last of his hot chocolate, "I'm not really interested in the same stuff as most kids my age. Like, they care about sports and video games, and I care about books and how things work."

"Nothing wrong with that. You'll find your people."

"You think so?"

"I know so. The world is full of people who care about books and how things work. You just have to find them."

Brian smiled. "Thanks, Aunt Brit. You always know what to say."

Hah!

When I dropped him off at home, Julie was in the garden, planting something that looked suspiciously like vegetables.

"Starting a garden?" I asked.

"Trying to. Brian's been asking if we can grow our own tomatoes, and I figure it can't be that hard, right?"

I looked at the neat rows of seedlings she'd planted. "Looks like you're off to a good start."

"We'll see. Brian's doing a research project on sustainable living for school, and he's convinced we should be more self-sufficient."

"That kid is going to change the world someday."

Julie smiled. "As long as he doesn't change it too much before I'm ready."

Driving home, I thought about Brian's comment about justice - how in mystery novels, the bad guys always got caught. It was a comforting fiction, the idea that wrongdoing was always punished and good always triumphed.

Real life was messier than that. Sometimes justice had to be created rather than waited for. Sometimes the only way to stop a bad person was to become something a little bad yourself.

But for kids like Brian, who still believed the world could be fair, maybe that was enough. Maybe protecting that kind of innocence was worth whatever it cost.

Thirty-Four

SUNDAY EVENING FOUND US sitting around Joe's dining room table, the late afternoon light streaming through the windows. Marsha had outdone herself with dinner - herb-crusted salmon, roasted vegetables, and a salad with some kind of amazing vinaigrette that I was definitely going to ask for the recipe.

"This is incredible, Marsha," Stu said, taking another bite of salmon. "What's in this crust?"

"Dill, parsley, and a little lemon zest. The trick is mixing it with panko breadcrumbs instead of regular ones."

Joe reached over and squeezed her hand. "She's been perfecting that recipe for months. I've been the very willing taste tester."

The conversation flowed easily over dinner. Joe told us about a particularly challenging surgery he'd had that week - a reconstruction case that had required innovative techniques. Marsha shared updates about her nonprofit work, including a new program they were developing for job training.

"We're trying to help abuse survivors learn practical skills for rebuilding their lives," she explained. "Not just therapy, but actual tools they can use to become financially independent."

"That sounds amazing," I said, genuinely impressed. "What kind of skills?"

"Computer literacy, resume writing, interview techniques. A lot of these women have been isolated for years. They need confidence as much as they need training."

It was exactly the kind of work that mattered, and I could see why Marsha was passionate about it. After everything I'd seen in my own experiences, the idea of actually helping people heal and rebuild resonated deeply.

Over dessert - my chocolate cake, which disappeared quickly - the conversation took a more personal turn.

"Actually, Britney," Marsha said, setting down her fork, "I was hoping I could ask you for some advice. Joe thought you might have a good perspective on something I'm dealing with."

"Of course. What's going on?"

Marsha glanced at Joe, who nodded encouragingly. "It's about Melissa. We've been together for two years now, and lately she's been. . . different. Distant. She says it's work stress, but I think there's something else going on."

I felt a familiar tingle of attention. "Different how?"

"She's not sleeping well. Sometimes I wake up and find her sitting in the living room at three in the morning, just staring out the window. When I ask what's wrong, she says she's fine, but clearly she's not."

Joe leaned forward. "Marsha's worried, and I told her you might have some insight. You're good at reading people."

"Has she seemed scared of anything? Or anyone?" I asked carefully.

Marsha's expression sharpened. "That's exactly it. She's scared, but she won't tell me of what. I thought we trusted each other completely."

"Sometimes people keep secrets to protect the people they love," I said.

"That's what Joe said. But it's driving me crazy. Last week I suggested we take a vacation, maybe go somewhere relaxing, and she practically had a panic attack. Said she couldn't leave town right now."

Stu and I exchanged a glance. "Do you think she might be in some kind of trouble?" he asked.

"I don't know. Maybe? Her work has been really demanding lately, lots of late nights and weekend calls. She mentioned losing a big client recently - some publishing company. She seemed really upset about it, which isn't like her."

I kept my expression neutral, though my mind was racing. "That's rough. Losing a major client can be stressful."

"The thing is, she's never gotten this attached to work before. Usually when a client relationship ends, she just moves on to the next one. But this time. . . it's like she took it personally."

We talked for another hour, with Marsha sharing more details about Melissa's recent behavior. The picture that emerged was of someone carrying a heavy burden, trying to protect her girlfriend from something she couldn't or wouldn't explain.

"I love her," Marsha said as we were getting ready to leave. "But I don't know how to help someone who won't tell me what's wrong."

"Maybe just being there is enough for now," I said. "Sometimes people need time to work through things on their own before they can share them."

"I hope so. I really hope so."

Driving home, Stu and I were both quiet, processing what we'd heard.

"Think it's connected to anything we should worry about?" he asked.

I thought about the different kinds of secrets people kept. Some secrets were selfish - ways to avoid consequences or maintain an image. But others were protective, shields meant to keep the people you loved safe from ugly truths.

"Probably not," I said. "Sounds like relationship stress. They'll figure it out."

But part of me wondered what kind of publishing company would cause that level of anxiety in someone. And why Melissa would be so afraid to leave town.

Some secrets, I decided, were meant to stay buried. At least for now.

The next day, however, I found myself thinking about Marsha's concerns about Melissa. Something about the situation bothered me - not in a dangerous way, just in a "this doesn't add up" way.

I decided to call Marsha back.

"Brit! I'm so glad you called. I've been thinking about our conversation last night."

"Me too. I was wondering - have you tried just asking Melissa directly what's going on? Sometimes people need permission to share what's bothering them."

"I have, but she just says everything's fine. Which clearly it's not."

"What if you approached it differently? Instead of asking what's wrong, maybe tell her you've noticed she seems stressed and ask if there's anything you can do to help."

Marsha was quiet for a moment. "That's actually really good advice. I think I've been so focused on getting answers that I haven't been focused on just being supportive."

"Sometimes that's all people need - to know someone's in their corner without having to explain everything."

"You're right. I'm going to try that approach tonight."

"And Marsha? Don't take it personally if she's not ready to share yet. Some people need time to process things before they can talk about them."

"Thank you, Brit. This really helps."

After we hung up, I felt good about the conversation. Sometimes the best way to help was just to listen and offer perspective, not to solve everyone's problems.

Whatever was going on with Melissa, she and Marsha would figure it out together. That's what healthy relationships looked like - two people supporting each other through difficult times.

Thirty-Five

Friday night meant girls' night, and this week Sarah had convinced us to try a new wine bar downtown. The place was trendy in that aggressive way that screamed "we're trying too hard," but the wine was good and the atmosphere was lively enough to make conversation easy.

"So I have news," Julie announced after we'd ordered our second round. "Good news, actually."

"Please tell me it's about that difficult client finally being reasonable," Sarah said.

Julie laughed. "Better than that. Brit's been talking about expanding the business, maybe opening a third location. We've been working on the numbers, and it looks like it's actually going to happen."

"Julie, that's fantastic!" I reached across the table to squeeze her hand. "You've been working so hard on that market analysis."

"The research shows there's definitely demand in the Clearwater area. Enough to justify a satellite office, anyway."

"You deserve this," I said, and meant it. Julie had been instrumental in growing the business over the past year, taking on more responsibility and showing real leadership skills.

"The best part is, it means I'll be managing the new location. More autonomy, better hours, and Cody and I can finally start putting serious money away for Brian's college fund."

Sarah raised her wine glass. "To Julie, who's going to kick ass in her new position."

We clinked glasses, and I felt that warm glow that comes from watching good things happen to good people. Julie had earned this promotion through hard work and competence, not politics or luck.

"How's Brian taking the news?" I asked.

"He's excited, but also worried that I'll be working even more hours. I promised him that won't happen. This position actually has better work-life balance, since I'll be managing accounts rather than scrambling to fill last-minute requests."

"Smart kid to think about that," Sarah said.

"Too smart, sometimes. He asked if the promotion meant we could afford to go to that science camp he wants to attend this summer. I had to explain that the raise doesn't take effect until next quarter."

"What science camp?" I asked.

"Some program at USF that focuses on environmental science. It's exactly the kind of thing he'd love, but it's expensive. Maybe next year."

I made a mental note to look into the camp. If it was something Brian really wanted and money was the only obstacle, maybe I could help make it happen. He was a good kid who deserved opportunities to explore his interests.

The conversation shifted to Sarah's latest dating adventures, which were both entertaining and slightly horrifying. She had a talent for finding men who seemed normal at first but turned out to have bizarre quirks or deal-breaking flaws.

"This one seemed perfect," she was saying. "Good job, nice smile, could hold an actual conversation about books. So we go out to dinner, everything's going great, and then he starts explaining his theory about how the government is putting mind-control chemicals in tap water."

"Please tell me you didn't finish the date," Julie said.

"I finished my wine and then claimed a family emergency. Which wasn't entirely a lie, since my sanity is related to me and it was definitely in emergency mode."

I laughed, but part of me felt bad for Sarah. She was genuinely looking for someone to build a life with, but the dating pool in Tampa seemed to be full of people who looked normal on the surface but had serious issues underneath.

Kind of like me, I thought, then pushed the idea away. This wasn't the time for that kind of self-reflection.

We stayed at the wine bar until they started giving us pointed looks about closing time, then walked to our cars in that slightly wobbly way that comes from good wine and better friendship.

"Thanks for tonight," Julie said as we reached my Jeep. "I needed this. It's been a stressful few weeks."

"The promotion stress or regular life stress?"

"Both. Brian's been asking questions about his father lately, and I don't know how to handle it."

That was new. In all the years I'd known Julie, Brian had never shown much curiosity about his absent father.

"What kind of questions?"

"Basic stuff. What was he like, why isn't he around, do I think they'll ever meet. I've been honest that his father wasn't ready to be a parent, but Brian's getting old enough to want more details."

"That's tough."

"The thing is, I don't want to poison Brian against his father, but I also don't want to paint him as some romantic figure who'll come back someday. His father made it clear he didn't want to be involved, and that's not going to change."

I thought about my own father, who'd been physically present but emotionally absent for most of my childhood. Sometimes having a parent who didn't want to be there was worse than having no parent at all.

"Brian's got a good head on his shoulders," I said. "Whatever you tell him, he'll handle it."

"I hope so. I just don't want him to feel like he's missing something essential, you know?"

"He's not. He's got you, and Joe, and all of us who love him. Family isn't just biology."

Julie smiled. "When did you get so wise?"

"Must be all those self-help books Brian keeps recommending."

We hugged goodbye, and I drove home feeling grateful for the people in my life. It was easy to take friendships for granted, but nights like this reminded me how lucky I was to have found my chosen family in Tampa.

Some people spent their whole lives looking for the kind of connections I'd stumbled into almost by accident. Maybe that was what happiness really looked like - not grand gestures or dramatic moments, but quiet Friday nights with people who knew your stories and cared about your future.

Thirty-Six

THE SCIENCE CAMP THING kept bothering me, so Monday morning I called USF to get more information about their summer environmental science program for kids.

"It's a two-week intensive," the coordinator explained. "We cover everything from marine biology to climate science to sustainable technology. The kids love it because it's all hands-on learning - field trips, lab work, actual research projects."

"And the cost?"

"Eight hundred dollars, which includes all materials and field trip transportation. We do offer some partial scholarships based on need."

I thought about Julie's excitement over her promotion, and how carefully she'd had to explain to Brian that they couldn't afford the camp yet. Eight hundred dollars wasn't a huge amount for me, but for a single mom trying to save for college, it might as well be eight thousand.

"What's the application deadline?"

"We're still accepting applications for this summer. The program runs in July."

After I hung up, I sat at my desk thinking. There were ways to help without making it obvious. Julie was proud, and she'd never accept what felt like charity. But maybe there was a middle ground.

I pulled up the camp's website and found what I was looking for: a corporate sponsorship program. Businesses could sponsor kids in exchange for promotional consideration and tax benefits.

Perfect.

I called back and spoke to the development office about having Passing Through sponsor a student. They were delighted - apparently corporate sponsors were rare for the summer programs.

"We'd be happy to set that up," the development coordinator said. "Do you have a specific student in mind?"

"Brian Morrison. I believe his mother works for one of our client companies."

It wasn't technically a lie. Julie's company had used our services before, just not recently.

"Wonderful. We'll send you the paperwork, and you can decide how much recognition you'd like. Some sponsors prefer to remain anonymous."

"Anonymous would be fine."

By Wednesday, it was all arranged. Brian would receive a "scholarship" from an "anonymous corporate sponsor" that would cover the full cost of the camp. Julie would never know it came from me, and Brian would get his environmental science adventure.

I was feeling pretty good about the whole thing when Stu came home that evening with news of his own.

"Remember how I put in for that detective position?" he said, loosening his tie.

"Of course. Did you hear something?"

"I got it. Detective Stuart Jones, at your service." He grinned. "Start date is next month."

I threw my arms around him. "Stu, that's incredible! I'm so proud of you."

"Thanks. It's going to be a big change - different hours, different kind of work. But I'm ready for it."

"What kind of cases will you be working?"

"Property crimes mostly, at least to start. Burglary, theft, fraud. Nothing too exciting, but it's good experience."

I thought about all the skills Stu had developed over the years - observation, investigation, reading people. He'd be a natural at detective work, even if he'd never know how much of his training had come from our extracurricular activities.

"When do you want to celebrate?" I asked.

"How about dinner at that steakhouse you like? The one with the ridiculous wine list?"

"Perfect. I'll make reservations."

We spent the evening planning how his schedule change would affect our routines. Detective work meant more regular hours than patrol, which would actually give us more time together. It felt like everything in our lives was moving in a positive direction.

Later, as we were getting ready for bed, Stu asked, "Any regrets about how we met?"

It was an odd question, but I knew what he was getting at. Our relationship had started during one of the darkest periods of my life, built on a foundation of shared secrets and mutual understanding of each other's capacity for violence.

"No regrets," I said. "Why?"

"Sometimes I wonder if we would have found each other under normal circumstances. If we'd met at a coffee shop or through friends, instead of..."

"Instead of during a murder investigation?"

"Yeah."

I thought about it. Stu without the darkness, me without the secrets we shared. Would we have recognized each other as kindred spirits? Would there have been the same immediate understanding, the same sense of finding someone who truly saw you?

"I don't know," I said honestly. "But I'm glad we don't have to find out. We found each other the way we found each other, and it worked."

Stu smiled and pulled me closer. "It definitely worked."

As I fell asleep that night, I felt grateful for the strange twists of fate that had brought us together. Some love stories started with meet-cutes and cute dates. Ours started with murder and mutual recognition of each other's monsters.

But somehow, it had led us to this: a normal Tuesday night in a normal house, talking about promotions and dinner plans like any other couple. Maybe that was the real miracle - not that we'd found each other, but that we'd found a way to build something healthy from such dark beginnings.

Thirty-Seven

THREE MONTHS LATER, I was standing in my kitchen on a Saturday morning, making coffee and watching Stu read the newspaper at our table. Detective work suited him - he'd solved four major cases in his first quarter and earned a commendation from the captain. More importantly, he seemed genuinely happy with the work.

"Anything interesting in there?" I asked, settling into the chair across from him with my mug.

"The usual. City council drama, high school football scores, someone complaining about construction noise." He folded the paper and set it aside. "Actually, there is something I wanted to talk to you about."

"Good something or bad something?"

"Good something. Great something, actually." He reached across the table and took my hand. "I've been thinking about what we talked about a few months ago. About making this official."

"The wedding?"

"I think we should do it. Soon. Before we get caught up in work again and another year passes."

I felt a flutter of excitement mixed with nervousness. We'd been engaged for years now, but between building the business and Stu's career change, we'd kept putting off actual planning.

"How soon are we talking?"

"Spring? March or April, maybe. Small ceremony like we discussed. Just the people who matter most."

I thought about it. Joe and Marsha, Julie and Cody and Brian, Barb and Jim, maybe a few others. The kind of intimate celebration that actually meant something instead of a big production for people we barely knew.

"I love that idea," I said. "But I have one condition."

"Name it."

"No white dress. I refuse to be a hypocrite about purity symbolism."

Stu laughed. "Deal. What about blue? You look incredible in blue."

"Blue works."

We spent the next hour sketching out rough plans. My backyard for the ceremony, catering from that little Italian place we loved, Marsha's nonprofit friend who was an ordained minister. Simple, personal, perfect.

The conversation was interrupted by my phone ringing. Julie's name on the screen.

"Hey, how's Brian doing at camp?"

"That's actually why I'm calling. They want to extend his stay another two weeks. Apparently, he's been such an asset to the research project that they're offering him a junior researcher position for the rest of the summer."

"That's incredible! He must be thrilled."

"Over the moon. But here's the thing - there's an additional cost for the extended program. The scholarship covers the original session, but not the extra time."

I was already reaching for my checkbook before she finished the sentence. "How much?"

"Brit, I can't ask you to—"

"You're not asking. I'm offering. Brian deserves this opportunity."

"You've already done so much. The original scholarship, all the support you've given our family. . ."

"Julie, stop. This is what family does for each other. How much?"

She told me the amount, and I promised to have a check in the mail that afternoon. It wasn't about the money—it was about making sure a good kid got to follow his passion without his parents having to choose between his future and their rent.

After I hung up, Stu was smiling at me. "You're a good person, you know that?"

"I'm selfish. Making Brian happy makes me happy."

"If that's selfish, the world needs more selfishness like yours."

The rest of Saturday was spent on wedding planning and household projects. We measured the backyard for seating, called vendors for quotes, and started a guest list. Normal domestic activities that felt surprisingly satisfying.

Sunday brought an unexpected visitor. I was working in the garden when a car pulled into our driveway. Marsha got out, looking unusually serious.

"Hey," I said, pulling off my gardening gloves. "Everything okay?"

"Actually, yes. Better than okay. I wanted to thank you."

"For what?"

"For the advice about Melissa. You were right about giving her space to share when she was ready."

I led her to the patio chairs, curious about where this was going. "What happened?"

"She finally told me what was going on. That publishing client she lost? It wasn't just a business relationship ending. The company was involved in some kind of research that made her uncomfortable, and when she tried to pull out, they threatened her."

I felt a chill. "Threatened her how?"

"Legal action, professional sabotage, making sure she couldn't work in Tampa. She was terrified, but she felt like she couldn't tell me because she didn't want to drag me into it."

"And now?"

"The company folded. Went out of business suddenly about a month ago. Melissa says the pressure just. . . stopped. Like whatever they were worried about became irrelevant."

I kept my expression neutral, though my mind was racing. "That's good. She must be relieved."

"She is. We both are. But I wanted you to know that your advice made all the difference. Instead of pushing for answers, I just focused on being supportive. When she was ready to talk, she knew I was there for her."

After Marsha left, I sat on the patio thinking about the conversation. Synergy Publishing had folded. Erika Logan's operation had collapsed, and Melissa was free from whatever hold they'd had over her.

I wondered what had caused Erika to shut down so suddenly, but decided I didn't really want to know. Some questions were better left unasked.

Stu came outside with two glasses of wine and settled into the chair next to me.

"Good visit with Marsha?"

"Apparently Melissa's work situation resolved itself. The company that was giving her problems went out of business."

"That's convenient timing."

"Very convenient."

We sat in comfortable silence, watching the sun set over Tampa Bay. The same view we'd enjoyed dozens of times, but it never got old. There was something peaceful about endings - the day ending, problems resolving themselves, threats disappearing into the past.

"You know what I realized today?" Stu said.

"What's that?"

"This is the longest I've ever gone without anything dramatic happening in my life. No family crises, no work disasters, no relationship problems. Just. . . normal life."

"Is that good or bad?"

"It's perfect. I never knew how much I wanted ordinary until I had it."

I understood exactly what he meant. There had been a time when I'd thrived on chaos and danger, when the adrenaline of hunting predators had felt like the only thing that made me feel alive. But this quiet contentment was better than any high I'd ever experienced.

"I love our ordinary life," I said.

"Even when ordinary includes wedding planning and mortgage payments and whose turn it is to clean the bathroom?"

"Especially then."

Stu reached over and took my hand. "I like the sound of Mr. and Mrs. Cage."

"I'm keeping my name."

"Even better. Detective Jones and Ms. Cage sounds pretty badass."

As the last light faded from the sky, I thought about the future we were planning together. A wedding in the spring, maybe a honeymoon somewhere quiet and beautiful. Growing the business, supporting the people we cared about, building something lasting and good.

It wasn't the life I'd planned when I was younger, but it was the life I'd chosen. Every decision I'd made, every path I'd taken, had led me here. To this house, this man, this peaceful evening on our patio.

My phone buzzed with a text notification. I glanced at it, expecting something from Julie or Barb about work.

Instead, it was from an unknown number: *Enjoyed our coffee chat. Looking forward to working together soon. - E.L.*

I stared at the screen, my blood cooling. Erika Logan. The woman who'd approached me months ago, whose company had supposedly folded, who should have been out of my life completely.

"Everything okay?" Stu asked, noticing my expression.

"Work thing," I said, deleting the message. "Nothing urgent."

But it wasn't nothing. Erika Logan was still out there, still playing games, still thinking she was clever enough to manipulate me. Marsha might be free from whatever hold Synergy had over Melissa, but that didn't mean Erika was done.

Some people spent their whole lives searching for excitement and adventure. I'd found something better—a life worth protecting, people worth loving, and the quiet satisfaction of becoming someone I could respect.

The monsters were gone, defeated or fled or simply irrelevant.

Except for one.

I looked at Stu, peaceful and content in the fading light, and made a decision. This life we'd built, this happiness we'd found - I'd do anything to protect it.

Even if it meant becoming a monster myself one more time.

Welcome to my list, Erika. Hope you enjoyed that text.

Because it might be your last.

Also by Amanda Byrd

13 Reasons for Murder:
Politeness Kills (#1)
Meathead (#2)
Philistines (#3)
Hungry (#4)
Bad Blood (#5)
Betrayal (#6)
Disillusioned (#7)
Harlot (#8)
Haunt (#9)

The Morgan Davis Serials
The Girl at the Bottom of the Ocean (#1)
Before You Die (#2)

Serial Women of History
Amelia Earhart, Serial Killer

Acknowledgments

This book, let alone series, wouldn't be possible without the following people and references:

Practical Homicide Investigation (5th Edition) by way of a Thomas Harris acknowledgement. The FBI's *Serial Murder Multi-Disciplinary Perspectives for Investigators* Report (available free online), and *psychologytoday.com* for helping me add the necessary depth to Britney.
Ret. Sgt. Chuck Burns for his consultation where the textbook didn't answer specific questions.

Justin D., for helping me on ridiculously short notice with some nicknames.

Nathan, for his advice and invitations. I'm so very grateful I finally decided to take you up.

Mark…sweet Mark. Without you, I wouldn't be here. I love you more than I can express and always will.

Jason, for the awesome editing and blurbs and feedback and advice and just being you. You have made me the writer I am today. Let's not get arrested, please. At least not before we make that money.